I AM
Mr. Bowersox

Readers said...

There can never be too many stories that immerse us into the lives and plight of horses in our society. "I am Mr. Bowersox" is one of those important stories that although is part fiction and part fact, depicts a reality faced by far too many horses. This story will help readers of all ages understand that commitment to owning and caring for a horse needs to be a commitment for a lifetime, insuring that even if you can no longer care for your horse, it is our responsibility as an owner and a society to make sure that all horses have the care they need. Thousands of nameless horses that arrive at auction had a Catherine in their past. Few find a White Bird Appaloosa Horse Rescue.

Daryl Tropea, Senior Deputy Director, The Global Federation of Animal Sanctuaries

Human beings lose their way in this story, but never Mr. Bowersox. Even as he loses love, his home, friends, suffers from starvation and taunting, even when he's nameless, blind, and unwanted in the back lot of the stockyard -- he remembers who he Is – "I AM strong, brave, clever, a good boy." Too often people forget these virtues and unfortunate animals, like Mr. Bowersox, suffer from our moral laziness and mistakes. Fortunately, several people in this true story are as awesome as this pony, people like his brave rescuers, Jeff and Virginia, and all his kind caretakers at White Bird. Wise and bittersweet, Mr. Bowersox shows us what every equine is made of -- dignity. Let's hope that human beings follow his heroic example.

Deborah Slicer, Ph.D., UVA; M.F.A., UVA; Professor of Philosophy, University of Montana, College of Humanities and Sciences

A lovely story for younger readers, which follows the life and times of a brave, little pony called Mr. Bowersox. What makes this story so unusual and special among equine based literature is that it is written from the horse's viewpoint. So we get to hear what the little pony is thinking, and how he feels about the people he meets and the situations he encounters - something we would love to hear from our own horses! There's even a delightful twist at the end, which I won't spoil for you...and a reminder too that there's always a special place in our hearts for those that we love.

Mark Mottershead - Founder, HorseConscious.com

I AM
Mr. Bowersox

by
Jorg Huckabee-Mayfield

All net proceeds from the sale of this publication will be donated for the care of rescued horses at the White Bird Appaloosa Horse Rescue.

First Paperback Edition: September 2015
Printed in the United States of America
ISBN: 978-0-9968044-1-7
Cover design by Alexandra Lopez-Cuadra

Acknowledgements

To Jeff and Virginia Hudson, without whom this book could not have been written. I also wish to thank Rabiah Seminole, for her kind encouragement and selfless efforts to help homeless horses. The backbone of any rescue organization is its people, and I wish to express my deep gratitude to the volunteers of the White Bird Appaloosa Horse Rescue, who have worked so hard to provide a safe haven for Mr. Bowersox and countless other horses over the years. Most of all, my thanks to Tom, for making it possible for White Bird's rescued horses to spend the remainder of their lives in safety and dignity.

Jorg Huckabee-Mayfield

"One's philosophy is not best expressed in words; it is expressed in the choices one makes...and the choices we make are ultimately our responsibility."

Eleanor Roosevelt

Jorg Huckabee-Mayfield

Table of Contents

Jorg Huckabee-Mayfield

Author's Note

Mr. Bowersox was real. He was run through the Missoula, Montana, livestock auction in October 2010. Starved and blind, he failed to receive even the lowest bid of $1, at which point his owner simply abandoned him. The horse he arrived with was sold to a slaughter buyer.

We do not know the details of Mr. Bowersox's earlier life. But we know certain things about him. We know that he had a strong sense of who he was, and that he associated very strongly with people. We also know that ponies can live a long time, and that as they age, they can pass through many hands. If they develop a health issue or, like many Appaloosas, lose their vision, they can lose their value and eventually become worthless to their owners. So, while the first part of his story is fiction, it is based on our knowledge of many ponies just like him that have endured a similar trajectory. What ultimately happened to Mr. Bowersox is an amazing story in itself—and it is true.

When people buy horses for themselves or their children, they typically expect to keep them until they no longer ride or their children outgrow them. They often do not realize that their pony can live to be forty years old. Today, horse rescues are full of aged horses and ponies that once had owners who cared deeply about them. But by the time of their rescue, these horses often have suffered terribly.

Many never make it to rescues at all, dying quietly from neglect, unseen and unmourned. The pony Allison was real and her story is true, too. Unfortunately, stories like these are all too common.

According to statistics compiled by the Equine Welfare Alliance, some 152,814 American horses were exported for the slaughter market in 2013, primarily to Mexico, Canada, and Japan. Until we close our borders to this industry, horses will continue to die in foreign slaughterhouses.

If I accomplish anything with this book, I hope it will be to make people think carefully before they discard the pony that no one else will love as much as they have, and that they have not loved enough to keep safe.

JHM

September 15, 2015

The soft creaking of the stable door tells me that the wind has changed direction. Now fully awake, I hear the faint rustling of leaves. The cool breeze brushes my forelock, and I lift my nose into the air to smell. Winter will be here soon.

I am Mr. Bowersox. I am old now, over forty. So many things have happened that I must remember each thing by itself, in its own place in my memory. Some of those things were terrible and some of them wonderful. But each led to another, until they made up the whole, long life that brought me here. I close my eyes, and I am back at the beginning, so many years ago.

Chapter 1

Big Chief

A shriek pierced the night like an arrow, and I opened my eyes for the first time.

"Looks like Minnie's had her foal," uttered soft voices. They were barely discernable.

Minnie was my mother. She was called Minnie because she was black with white socks, and when she was born, the girls thought she looked like Minnie Mouse.

"He's a colt, sort of small but seems strong enough. And look—he's an Appaloosa!"

I was introduced to the world one spring in the chill hours of early morning. I was cold and frightened but soon was comforted by the soft nuzzling of my mother, who urged me to my feet. At first, the world spun in circles. Everything was blurry, and my legs didn't know exactly where to go. But I soon got the hang of standing and began to take my first steps, as my mother gently insisted. She showed me where to find breakfast, and I drank the sticky, warm milk until my belly could hold no more.

Around us in the pre-dawn light were the soft outlines of my herd. I could hear them grazing: the first squeak of their teeth across the grass, then the quick tearing sound, and finally a comforting, slow munch. Occasionally, a contented snort would interrupt this rhythm. As the sky lightened, I could see that we were in a valley, surrounded by tall, gray mountains with snowy peaks. Along the valley floor, the snow had melted. The ground was covered with brilliant green, dotted with the blooms of small wildflowers. A bold stream ran down its center.

My aunts, cousins, and sisters surrounded me. My father stood some distance away, head held high, scanning the area intently—watching, listening, and smelling for any sign of danger. He was a powerful old stallion with a dark gray coat and many scars. He was fierce and intimidating.

The milk soon had its effect, and suddenly I was full of energy. I wanted to run and jump! After a few wobbly starts, I began sprinting in small circles around my mother. She watched for several minutes and then trotted away slowly. I trotted with her, feeling the wind in my face and the strength building in my legs. And then, we were off! We raced across the valley floor. I leapt and jumped. I whirled and whinnied at the top of my voice. The older horses looked on, fascinated and amused. Even the old stallion softened for a moment, lowering his head to watch.

We circled back to the herd. As soon as we slowed to a stop, I was suddenly very tired. I collapsed onto the ground and immediately fell asleep, my mother standing over me.

I awakened to the sound of voices. The sun had arisen fully, and the hood of a pickup truck parked by the road glistened brightly. A man and two girls stood near my family, and I knew they were watching me. Because my family generally ignored the onlookers, only watching them obliquely out of one eye, I knew they were not to be feared. My mother was still cautious, keeping me on her other side in case anyone moved toward us.

"He's got spots. I guess they call that a 'few spot' Appaloosa. He's got dark legs, too. They sometimes call that color 'pewter.' He's a cute little booger. Too bad about his size."

"He's okay, Pa. He'll get big enough for me to train, anyway," said the older of the two children, a slender teenage girl wearing a brown coat with a furry collar. From behind my mother, I peeked out to see the younger daughter, a small child with tousled hair and huge brown eyes, hands stuffed into her pockets for warmth. She gazed at me, her face a picture of complete fascination.

That night, I awoke to a shrill scream of pain and the panicked rush of horses. I could smell fear in the air, and something faintly metallic. We ran in the darkness, my mother beside me, enveloped in the thunderous rush of the herd. My father ran behind us, driving us forward, urging us to run quickly. We reached the top of the hill and stood gazing at the landscape below, nostrils flaring, ears alert. My father arrived last, limping and with an open wound visible on one leg. He had bravely run behind the herd, placing himself in harm's way. Everyone was nervous. We stood there for hours, my family grazing around me, occasionally snapping their heads up at a suspicious sound or smell. One chestnut mare stood slightly apart from the group, nickering softly into the darkness.

Early the next morning, the man and the older girl came back.

"Mountain lion," the man concluded. "That was pretty bold, but I guess they're hungry after the long winter. That was going to be a nice colt, too. Let's bring them in to finish foaling out."

"Hope old Beans is okay," said the girl.

Later that day, the pair appeared on horses I didn't recognize. They rode up behind us and began to swing lariats, shouting and whistling, coming up quickly in a way that made everyone uncomfortable. We moved forward while Beans anxiously assumed his place behind the herd, in effect joining the effort.

We walked for over an hour down the valley, parallel to the stream. Finally, as we rounded a low hill, we could see a ranch laid out before us. A house sat at its center, surrounded by fields, fences, and buildings. Some of the fields held cattle, which eyed us curiously as we passed. When we reached the pasture closest to the house, we walked through the gate. The man dismounted, closing it behind us. My family was relaxed and comfortable; they knew this place well. They dropped their heads and began to graze.

I, on the other hand, was keen to explore. I trotted first around my mother, then my aunts, never straying too far but determined to see, hear, and smell absolutely everything. Every so often, I raced back to hide behind my mother, just in case.

A door slammed. I looked in the direction of the house to see the younger girl running toward the fence, a worried frown on her face. Arriving at the fence, she scanned the group anxiously.

"He got another one of the foals," her father said quietly.

"Not Minnie's!" She gasped and threw her hands to her mouth in horror.

"No, he's okay. Looks like it was Gracie's."

The young girl exhaled and craned her neck, searching intently until her eyes finally rested on me. "Whew! Big Chief is okay."

"Big Chief? That's a pretty grandiose name for half a horse. How about something more appropriate, like 'Half Pint'?"

The other girl chimed in, a mischievous grin on her face. "How about 'Short Stuff' or 'Stubby' or...'Mini Minnie'!" She cracked up, making the shape of a small horse with her hands.

The little girl threw out her chest and defiantly put her hands on her hips. "He's Big Chief, and he is going to be beeoootiful!"

So, Big Chief it was, shortened later to just "Chief." We stayed in that pasture for months. The man and the girls checked on us frequently, walking among the horses and talking to us softly in low, reassuring tones. Occasionally, they paused to stroke a neck or rub a friendly forehead. On some mornings, I awoke to find new, bright-eyed foals just meeting the world.

At first, Catherine, the younger girl, kept her distance from my mother and me, knowing instinctively that my mother would be protective. But this concern soon faded, and Catherine came closer and closer as I grew stronger and my mother relaxed. Some days, Catherine just sat next to us in the grass, telling us about her cat, stories about dolls, or whatever else was on her mind.

One day, she slowly stretched out her hand and placed it on my neck. Surprised, I jumped away at the strange touch. But seconds later I came back to sniff this strange appendage, and when it touched me again, I stood still. Catherine gently rubbed my neck and mane. I started to protest, but I had to admit that it felt pleasant. I soon learned to relax and enjoy my friend's affectionate rubs and scratches.

Our family was not large compared to some herds. We were only seven mares and five foals, in addition to Beans. Of the foals, myself included, two were colts and three were fillies. My family trusted people, and we were treated well. When, one day, the man and two girls came out and began to lead Beans and the mares into the next field, we felt no reason to worry. But the gate closed behind each horse, eventually leaving just the foals in a small group on one side, with the adult horses on the other.

When we realized what was happening, our moms called out to us, pacing worriedly along the fence line. We whinnied and dashed about, trying to find a way back to our moms. I could see the dark shape of my mother anxiously testing the fence for weak spots or openings. We called out and whinnied until we were exhausted, and then we whinnied some more. The father, Catherine, and her older sister Abby all stood nearby, watching solemnly as we called out to each other.

"I hate weaning!" Catherine cried out, never taking her eyes off me. "You'll be okay, Big Chief. I promise."

After several days, we realized we would be okay. Our mothers could see us over the fence, and we were comforted by their presence. The father, Catherine, and Abby brought buckets of weanling food so delicious that we ate it all and wanted more. Over time, we learned to wear halters, to lead and tie, and to pick up our feet when asked. We grew more independent, worrying less about our moms and spending more time playing.

We raced each other. We played "Who's the biggest stallion?" We play fought, nipping and kicking each other. Sometimes, we reached over each other's necks to scratch our teeth along another's withers—the very best feeling in the world. As we grew stronger, the fillies became more interesting to the colts, giving us strange new stirrings, as well as the seeds of mistrust between each other. We began to play rough.

One day, a new truck came, and a different man met Catherine and her father.

"Morning, Jim," said the stranger, as the two adults shook hands.

"Those two youngsters over there, Dr. Burke," Jim responded, pointing in our direction.

"No! No! No!" Catherine erupted. She tearfully tried to hold back her father, clinging to his hand and digging her heels into clumps of grass.

"Now Catherine, you know we have to do this."

"But it's going to hurt!"

Catherine's father stopped walking and crouched down to face her. "But it won't," he assured her. "I promise you, he won't feel anything. And you know I never break a promise. You'll see. Okay?"

After a moment, she slowly nodded her head up and down, then wiped her nose on the back of her sleeve. The pair stood up, and the group resumed walking toward us. Catherine took the halter, approached me, and fastened it around my head. She snapped the lead onto it, just as we had done hundreds of times before. As the two men stood next to me, a bee stung my neck. I flinched but was oddly comfortable. Warmth flowed through my body. I was suddenly very sleepy and couldn't keep my balance.

I felt the warm sun as I nibbled the grass in front of me. I was lying on my chest, my legs tucked to the side. I could not remember how I had gotten there. I felt vaguely sleepy, but good.

"You see?" the father explained. "He's so young that this isn't a big deal for him. We can't have more than one stallion, and he'll be a lot happier and calmer if he doesn't have to worry about where the mares are and whether Beans is going to beat the snot out of him." He looked down at the ground, trying to hide the amusement on his face. "He's not exactly executive material, anyway."

Catherine sighed as she stroked my neck with her small fingers. "I guess. You okay, Big Chief?" I was.

After that, the years flew by. I grew bigger and stronger, though never as big as my parents or siblings. But I knew that I was clever and brave—and that Catherine loved me more than anyone or anything in the world.

Chapter 2

Good, Clever, and Brave

When I was about five years old, Abby began to teach me to carry a rider. Up to this point, she had taught me many other things in preparation. She would lead me into the round pen, say a word, and then show me with her body (or sometimes a long whip or rope), what she wanted me to do.

I tried hard to figure out the meaning of the word or motion, to discern the right thing to do. Sometimes, I guessed wrong. Each time, Abby patiently started over, repeating it until I got it right.

"Walk on!" she would command. Then she would step behind my shoulder, which made me want to step forward. As I did this, she would say, "Good boy," which always made me happy. If she wanted me to shift my hindquarters to the side, she would stand beside them and make a kissing noise so I would know to move my rear away from her.

I liked the training. We always started with a good grooming.

Catherine would brush my coat and check for any little cuts or bumps. By now, my hair was becoming lighter, not the darker gray coat I was born with. It was almost white, except for my legs and a few black spots. She brushed my tail until it flowed like silk. Like many Appaloosas, I didn't have much of a mane, so when she came to that, she just ruffled it and told me how handsome I was. She knew how to scratch that wonderful spot, just behind my withers.

Catherine would also pick up each foot to pull out small stones or dirt with a hoof pick, so I didn't risk bruising my feet. I enjoyed all this attention because I got to spend time with Catherine. She talked to me while she worked, telling me I was brave and strong.

When Abby and I trained, Catherine often hung on the rails of the round pen. As I would circle, I could hear her encouraging me softly: "Go on, Boy. Good job." On some lazy days I might have preferred grazing, but on most days I tried hard to be good. When we finished each lesson, Abby would hand the lead to Catherine to take me out. Catherine always gave me a big hug.

Abby and I practiced putting on the blanket, saddle, and bridle until these were comfortable and familiar to me. She leaned into the saddle to get me used to the feeling of weight on my back. When the day came that she finally slid into the saddle, it was the strangest feeling. I adjusted my weight to balance myself, but I wasn't sure what to do next. I tried to remember what she taught me—the words and the way her body put pressure on mine. I was very confused at first, but I tried to do things as we had practiced them. After a few tries, I started to get it right, and soon we were walking around the pen together. "Good boy," she said quietly.

I looked over to see Catherine's face, radiant with joy. She tried hard to hide her excitement, but I could see that she had trouble staying quiet. Though she desperately wanted to jump and whoop, all she said was, "I told you he was clever." I was so proud.

During that time, Jim and Abby trained my siblings, too. The father worked with the girls, now big and beautiful—and generally more opinionated about things. They were solid mares, not easily convinced to do as instructed. Abby also trained my half-brother. He was bigger than I was, but slower to learn, and a little grumpy.

These were good days. We were healthy, young horses in our prime who had learned to be willing partners with our human riders. When we were not practicing our new skills, we lived peacefully in our valley, grazing in lush meadows, surrounded by blue-gray mountains.

Late one summer morning, as my siblings and I grazed in the large paddock near the house, I heard the faint sound of a truck in the distance, the crunch of the tires on the gravel road growing progressively louder until a plume of dust appeared to formally announce our visitor. When the truck pulled to a stop, Jim walked up and greeted the driver, a pleasant man in a short-sleeved, plaid shirt. The pair approached us, and Jim began describing our ages and level of training. The man asked questions and Jim answered them, as they watched us relaxing by the fence.

"This bay mare has a nice shoulder and a short back. Look at that kind eye, too," Jim offered.

"Wasn't really considering a mare, but I might be persuaded," responded the visitor.

Meanwhile, Catherine sat stone-faced, trying not to look at me or anyone else. There was more back and forth discussion, with talk of mares being "marish" and the benefits of short pasterns and sloped shoulders. It was a verbal to and fro that included observations like, "She has a butt like a diesel tractor." Eventually, the two men shook hands. Catherine relaxed, a tiny "Yay!" escaping from under her breath. Later that day, a trailer pulled up and my half-sister walked up the ramp. The back door closed, and the trailer drove away.

The scenario repeated many times over the next few months. Sometimes no horse left, while other times people shook hands, and one of my siblings would go away in a trailer. Whenever a potential buyer arrived, Catherine became tense and sat silently, biting her lip—staying just close enough to hear every word of the conversation.

One day, Jim, Abby, and Catherine walked together to the paddock, near where I stood. As they walked, Jim and Abby exchanged glances, and I could sense that something was transpiring between the two. Catherine walked just a little ahead of them, as usual, eager to visit me and already reaching into her pocket for a treat.

When they reached the fence, Catherine offered me the carrot she had brought and rubbed my forehead as I crunched it noisily. But Abby was strangely quiet. Jim looked down at his younger daughter. "Cath, there's something we need to talk about."

"Yes, Pa?"

His face expressionless, he proceeded. "You know the cattle didn't bring much this year. I was hoping to have a little extra money, but instead we're going to have to tighten our belts. We'll need to make some sacrifices."

Her curiosity turned to concern. She waited.

"I'm afraid there isn't going to be much for your birthday this year."

Catherine let out a long sigh and nodded. Like many ranch children, she had heard this before.

"That's okay, Pa." She tried not to sound disappointed. Abby stared at the ground.

Her father scratched his chin and continued solemnly. "So, the only real choice I have is to give you Chief. So, happy birthday from me and Abby!" He broke into a huge grin. Abby looked up and smiled broadly.

It took a moment for the message to sink in. "Big Chief! For me?" Catherine shrieked and whooped, jumping up and down, first hugging her dad, then Abby, then racing over to bury her face in my neck.

Catherine had learned to ride nearly as early as she had learned to walk. This wasn't unusual for a rancher's daughter. But breaking and training horses was generally left to adults and older, more experienced children. Once horses were fairly well trained, children and less experienced riders could ride them. Days before, I had heard Abby telling her father that I was ready, but for what I did not know. Now, I did. I was ready for Catherine's eleventh birthday.

"Go on, then. Go saddle up your horse," her father said. Catherine let out another burst of excitement and giddily ran to the barn for the tack.

From that point on, Catherine and I were inseparable. Our home lay within a long valley, with mountains on both sides. In between the valley and the mountain peaks were vast pine forests, extending like green skirts around the base of the mountains, sometimes stretching far up the slopes.

Every day, when Catherine came home from school, we rode off on adventures. Sometimes, we walked beside the stream, looking for elk, bear, or bobcats. Other times, we meandered into the pines, spotting badgers, porcupines, and, sometimes, bighorn sheep. We raced along the valley bottom, feeling the wind in our faces, enjoying the sensation of going really, really fast. With my stout build, I was exceptionally strong and could climb a long way up the mountains, seldom tiring, with my friend on my back. We found secret places that no one else had probably ever seen. Sometimes, we went as high as we could go, rewarded with a panoramic view of the valley.

With practice, Catherine and I were nearly one. She could look in a direction, and I knew which way to go. Even a slight shift in her weight told me to go faster or slower, or to stop. When we galloped, we knew each other so well that we were in perfect balance—Catherine seemed to weigh nothing at all. Together, we flew like a single, large bird, gliding across the valley floor.

We got braver, wandering farther up the mountains and farther away from home. We once rode along the side of a jagged, rocky ridge in the higher elevations of pine forest. We'd been out for several hours, and Catherine knew I could use a rest and a drink of water. When we reached a small stream, she climbed down and led me to the edge of a pool so I could drink. She stood nearby on a large, flat rock, holding the reins as I lowered my head. All of a sudden, I smelled something I knew to be bad. I looked around anxiously. Just as Catherine turned and began to step off the rock, the faint outline of a coiled snake appeared in the shadow where her foot was descending.

I swung my head around quickly, and my neck caught her in the chest with a loud thud, knocking her backward. Small pebbles scattered in all directions as she landed. The movement startled the snake, which struck out with incredible speed. But there was no foot to bite. Catherine was several feet away, picking herself up and wondering what had happened. She didn't wonder for long. The snake, now in the open, coiled defensively. A familiar rattling sound filled the air. We both backed away. When the snake realized we had meant no harm, it quieted down and began to crawl back into the shadow of the rock.

Catherine stood for a few moments collecting herself, realizing how close we had come to a serious accident. We were miles away from help, and Prairie Rattlesnake venom is fast and lethal. As she regained her composure, she looked at me in slow amazement.

"You knew! How did you know that? How did you know what to do?"

The simple truth is that most horses don't like snakes. We fear them and either back away, or, if we think we are cornered, sometimes trample them. We can smell them, too, and many horses would have known the snake was there. But most simply would have moved away. I knew what to do because, as Catherine often said, I am clever. I acted as I did, because, as she also told me, I am brave.

Late one fall, we went out for a ride. It was a beautiful Saturday morning, and the air was crystal clear, bringing the mountains into sharp relief. Catherine had packed herself a picnic lunch that included an apple for me. By this time, we were going on very long rides, as we knew the mountains and surrounding country well. We often were gone the entire day. Catherine had become a skilled rider, and I was as strong a mountain pony as anyone could ask for.

We set off for the peaks and decided to take a high trail we had not visited in some time. The last time we had been there, we had seen a bear with two cubs, splashing and playing in a stream far below us. We rode for hours, exploring the terrain and enjoying each other's company. Catherine talked to me like the best friend that I was, telling me about the girls in her school and how she really didn't like her art teacher. As the morning turned to afternoon and the mountain shadows deepened, a shadow of a different sort approached rapidly from the west.

I recognized the heavy feel of snow in the air. I didn't mind snow. In fact, I liked to play in it, rolling back and forth and making horse "snow angels." I didn't think much about this change in weather. But I could tell that Catherine was uncomfortable. She had fallen silent and asked me to move faster as we headed toward home. But we were still hours away.

The squall hit us fast, accelerating quickly from a few tiny snowflakes to a solid white wall that surrounded us completely. Catherine slouched and kept her head down as the snow swirled and danced. The wind made a low moan as it traveled through the mountains. Within an hour, the ground was covered, and the snow began to drift. The landscape became different, unfamiliar.

I sensed Catherine's increasing concern, and I felt the tenseness in her body. After a while, she asked me to stop. She peered ahead. "This doesn't look right." She asked me to turn to the right, and I obeyed, stepping carefully down the slope. We traveled for another hour, and Catherine asked me to stop again. She looked around us, narrowing her eyes to see through the snow, but to no avail. She asked me to turn to the left, and I did. She was no longer only tense, she was cold, and she was beginning to shiver.

Finally, she asked me to stop. She chose her words carefully. She was so cold that they did not come easily to her. "Chief, I'm lost. I don't know which way to go. But I think you do. So, please take us home." With that, she dropped the reins and urged me forward. Without her direction, I did not understand where she wanted me to go. I took a few steps and waited. But she did not tell me. Instead, she urged me to go quickly. I felt her fear. It was late, and I wanted to go home. Guessing finally that this was her intent, I turned toward home.

We crossed deep drifts and walked around trees that had fallen under the weight of the snow. The landscape was hard to recognize. But I always knew exactly where I was. What I couldn't see, I could smell. When I couldn't identify my surroundings by smell, I could navigate by my internal compass, which always tells me where I am in the world. It took many more hours to get to the ranch, as the snow had slowed me down. At last, we could make out the halos of farm lights through the snow and darkness.

The horses in the paddocks announced our arrival with their usual greeting whinnies. I immediately heard shouts and smelled more horses—visitors from nearby who greeted us through the falling snow.

"Oh, thank God! Jim!"

"Catherine?"

A dozen faint shapes on horseback emerged from the gloom, some carrying lamps and flashlights. Catherine was too cold to talk. We rode toward the barn, lit brightly by lanterns. Once inside, Catherine slid off, nearly too stiff to walk. Abby and the visitors came in, too. The latter were neighbors and friends who had come from town. Their horses followed behind, now relaxed and glancing shyly at each other.

A friendly pinto gelding with ice in his mane leaned over and politely smelled my breath, while Catherine's father opened a metal container full of hot chocolate, insisting she drink. He hugged her for a long moment, rubbed her arms, and then thanked the now-cheerful visitors, wishing them a safe journey home. Meanwhile, I found some loose hay on the floor and settled down to eat. I was tired and hungry. The sounds of voices could be heard in the distance until they were drowned out by the rumble of engines coming alive. The trucks and trailers started for their homes.

As the last visitor was leaving, Catherine's father turned and asked, "Are you sure you're okay?" She nodded, then pulled the saddle and steaming blanket off my back.

"I'm lucky, though. We got lost in the snow, but Chief knew how to get us home. He is a good boy."

Chapter 3

Broken Promise

As the years sped by, Catherine grew taller. She began to look and sound less like a child and more like a young woman. She was quieter and had become involved in many things that did not involve me. I still waited for her every day after school, just in case, but more often than not, she came home with friends and remained inside the house. Her companions were girls about her age who had little interest in riding but could talk about makeup, clothes, and boys for hours at a time. I could hear them talking and giggling inside the house. The thump-thump-thump of rock music traveled far across the fields.

Sometimes, I could smell tobacco burning. One day, her father came home early and smelled it, too, and I heard angry shouts and the sound of doors slamming inside the house.

Catherine began to spend less time at home. When I did see her, she no longer looked like my girl. She smelled different, too, of soap and something like flowers but stronger and a little sour. Only occasionally did she come to visit me, and when she did, she rarely stayed for very long or had much to say. The rides we still took were short trips, and she barely spoke to me, as if I had become a stranger.

I knew I was losing my best friend. I missed her, but I did not know what to do. I did my best to behave and to show her that I was brave and clever, but this was not enough anymore. She was my only girl, the one I had loved since I was a foal and had come to know so well. Now, she did not even seem to notice me. My tail had become knotted, but there was no one to comb it out. My coat lost some of its shine, but no one brushed it. For the first time in my life, I was lonely. Her visits slowed to a trickle. Eventually, they stopped altogether.

One day, a brown, wood-paneled station wagon pulled up to the house, and Catherine and her father came out to greet the family that emerged, a man and woman and their three sandy-haired boys. The two parents listened while Catherine's father spoke, asking him occasional questions. The boys wandered off to explore the yard.

A short while later, Catherine, her father, and the two parents approached the paddock. The two older boys began to throw rocks into a puddle in the driveway, shouting excitedly when the muddy water splashed onto their trousers. The youngest of the three boys followed quietly behind his parents. When they reached the fence, the group stood looking at me. The smallest boy hung on the fence rail, sliding both feet over the lowest board as if he might slip in and join me, his shoelaces dangling haphazardly from unsecured sneakers.

"He's well broke and good with children," Catherine's father explained.

I did not understand. They continued looking at me and talking in low tones. I listened first in disbelief and then horror as the realization began to sink in. This could not be. I was Catherine's horse. They had said so. And Catherine's father never broke a promise. Unlike my siblings, I was a good boy. I was strong and clever, so I had not been sent away like the other horses. I looked anxiously at Catherine, but she seemed not to notice me. My heart raced, and my throat tightened.

"What'll you take for him?" The man asked.

I heard additional low conversation. Finally, the adults shook hands. The family piled back into the station wagon, the boys scuffling for position. I watched them drive all the way down the road until they disappeared from sight. This just could not be. Catherine and her father headed back to the house, their attention now on other matters.

Hours later, a pickup truck towing a small stock trailer arrived. My heart sank. I knew exactly what this meant. It meant that, this time, I would be going away. I did not know why or where—only that those horses never returned.

I waited for Catherine to tell the driver that this was all a big mistake and that I would not be sent away. But Catherine came over, slid a halter over my head and clipped the lead to it. She ran her hand across my forehead, pulling a stray bur from my forelock.

"Now, you be a good boy," she instructed.

We walked through the paddock gate. I never saw my home again.

Chapter 4

The Least of Their Concerns

We drove down out of the mountains until the Bitterroot Valley stretched wide in front of us. I could see the mountains in the distance, but we were lower, below the pines and looking out over an expanse of grassland. We had driven farther than I had ever traveled in one day. Finally, the trailer stopped, and I heard the rusty creak of the door opening behind me.

I carefully backed out and then looked around at my new home and the people who would be my new family. I introduced myself to the husband and wife who had brought me here. Meanwhile, the boys began to poke holes in the driveway mud with sticks.

"I am Big Chief. I am strong and brave and very clever. I am a good boy." But no one seemed to be paying any attention to me. Instead, the husband fumbled awkwardly with my lead, and we began to walk in the direction of the house.

The dwelling had cedar siding and a wide porch that faced the valley. Toys were strewn around the yard, including a bicycle with a bent wheel and the remains of a small tent, which had been shredded by the wind and now hung gloomily off a rope that sagged between two saplings. A nondescript, brown dog crossed the driveway, purposefully carrying a collapsed basketball in his mouth, as if he might bury it and eat it later. Aside from the dog, these were things I had never seen before, and they made me uncomfortable. As we walked past the house, I shied away from the strange objects, trying not to get too close in case one of them moved toward me.

Beside the house was a wide paddock made of wire fence and wood posts. On one side was a small stable. I was led through the gate and into the paddock. The boys' father unsnapped my lead, and I inspected the enclosure, checking first for dangerous things and then for an opening in the fence. I wanted to go home. But I was also hungry. Seeing no predators, I dropped my head to graze, but I remained alert for any sign of danger. I realized quickly that I was in someone else's yard. I could smell another horse, a mare, but could not see her, and that made me both anxious and excited.

The two adults stood against the fence watching me along with the youngest boy, who stood timidly holding his mother's hand. The older two boys had disappeared. "He sure seems quiet," the woman observed. "Robbie, doesn't he seem like a nice pony?" Robbie nodded solemnly.

I began to make my way down the fence line when, all of a sudden, I heard a shrill whinny. I snapped my head up and stared intently toward the origin of the sound. But I could not see another horse. I began to move in that direction—toward the stable—to investigate. As I approached, I finally made out the shape of the mare, but I could hardly believe my eyes.

Standing near the stable overhang was the smallest horse I had ever seen.

All the horses on my home ranch were taller than me. I had never looked down on an adult horse. This mare was smaller than most foals. Almost as small, in fact, as the dog I had just seen carrying the ball. She was as round as an apple, standing on short, stubby legs that almost disappeared beneath her belly. Her thick, blonde mane flew in all directions like an unruly haystack, and the tip of her tail dragged the ground. Her tiny body was a dappled chestnut and seemed to glow in the sunlight.

Not knowing what to make of her, I approached her cautiously— head down, to show that I was not a threat. I walked slowly so as not to frighten her. I knew that she might kick or bite me, or chase me away, as mares can be quite ferocious. But my caution was unnecessary. The little mare had begun to walk quickly toward me, and I heard her greet me with a throaty chuckle. I waited politely.

When she reached me, we introduced ourselves by smelling each other's breath. She did not squeal and jump, which she would have done to threaten me or warn me away. Rather, she arched her neck down and emitted a low rumbling from the back of her throat, an expression of pure good will. From beneath her thick forelock, a pair of bright eyes sparkled mischievously. She reached around to try to scratch my withers but was far too short. She instead settled for grooming my shoulder, raking her teeth across my skin in a satisfying scratch. In turn, I reached over and gently scratched her back. I had a friend.

I do not know what I would have done without Maggie. I was terribly homesick and longed to be back in my mountains. I still hoped Catherine would come get me and bring me home, though I knew inside that this was not to be.

Yet from the moment we met, Maggie and I were each other's very best friends. She had been alone for a long time, but now, we were rarely apart. We are herd animals, and we were each other's herd. We ate together, grazed together, and slept side by side. Sometimes in the evenings when the weather was cool, we raced around the paddock, kicking up our heels, pretending to run away from mountain lions. In cold weather, we stood under the overhang, staying close together for warmth. I loved her cheerful nature and her outsized personality. She was a big horse in a small body.

No one ever rode Maggie. Her tiny stature could not support the weight of even the youngest child. I was the pony that took them for rides, a gift from their parents. They called me "Jack."

The boys, aged six, nine, and ten, were named Robbie, Joe,

and Matt. None had much experience with horses other than Maggie. They were awkward and unbalanced, usually struggling to get onto my back and then shouting when they lost their balance and slid off. Each time, I repositioned myself and took care not to step on them accidentally. When they were able to stay on, we walked around the large paddock as I tried to keep them steady.

For the most part, they liked to play with me but had little interest in riding. They once put a hat over my ears and drew lips on my face with lipstick they had taken from their mother. They were silly and uninterested, preferring wrestling and combat games to ponies.

The remaining member of the family was Rufus, the dog I had seen with the basketball. Rufus seemed to be a mix of all breeds in one dog. He was quietly intelligent, and while he enjoyed the occasional attention of his family, he typically was more preoccupied with his own adventures. He always seemed to be on his way to doing something very important, and interruptions by the children were tolerated politely, but only briefly, before he continued on his way.

Their mother was called Helen, and she came out to feed us in the mornings. It was the boys' responsibility to feed us in the evenings. They usually remembered, but sometimes they forgot. I liked their mother. She was gentle and kind and spoke softly to us, sometimes bringing us apples or carrots. Every so often, she would take the body brush from the tack box in the corner and brush the mud out of our coats. Maggie sometimes snuck up behind Helen and thumped her in the leg with her head, knowing that Helen often carried treats in her pockets. Helen would laugh and then give us a snack or a pat, or tell us that we were unscrupulous beggars who should have real jobs. She liked being around us, and we enjoyed her company.

I also liked the youngest son, Robbie. He was a slender child who appeared constantly disheveled. There was something sad and different about him. But he was kind to us and would gently scratch our necks and rub our foreheads while we munched hay in the late afternoon sun.

Some days, when the boys were roughhousing, the two bigger boys would pile on top of Robbie, knocking him to the ground and pummeling him. He would protest and yell "Uncle!" and "I give up!" but the thrashing and shouting would continue until their father, from somewhere in the house, yelled, "You boys knock it off!"

The boys' father Dan was a big man with a ginger-colored beard and booming voice. He rarely came to visit us but was often nearby, splitting wood or bringing a load of hay to the stable. He usually wore an old felt cowboy hat and leather boots as big as Maggie's head. This apparel was occasionally complemented by a holster and large handgun, which he wore when he practiced target shooting at the edge of the woods. Sometimes, he threw footballs for the boys in the backyard. His deep "Go long!" seemed to carry for miles. We heard that same bellowing voice when the boys got too rambunctious and needed to settle down, especially when Robbie protested loudly.

Robbie tried to be a good sport with his older brothers. More than anything else, he wanted to please them, but he generally ended up the subject of their ribbing and taunts. When the play-fighting became rough, he would surrender and then dust himself off, laughing nervously. Helen watched all this uneasily, biting her lip and sometimes later giving Robbie a quiet hug of encouragement. We could see that she worried about her youngest son, but Dan brushed off her concerns. He often told his wife that they were "just being boys," and that he wished Robbie would stick up for himself.

Robbie spent more time by himself than either of the other two boys, who tended to stick together. Sometimes, he went off by himself to explore. Other times, he came to the stable to visit Maggie and me. He often snuck handfuls of grain to us when no one was watching. He would talk to us and brush us as we stood quietly, his small hands working through knots in our manes.

"Jack, you need to stop rolling in the mud. How are you supposed to stay clean?"

"Come here, Maggie. Your mane is a mess. Just look at you!"

Some days, he just sat silently next to us in the stable while we munched hay, closing his eyes and listening to the soft crunch, crunch, crunch. He seemed to feel safe in the peaceful environment of the stable.

One day, I noticed that he seemed to be listening intently to something. It was as if someone else was in the stable with us, someone neither Maggie nor I could see or hear. Occasionally, he nodded or fidgeted uncomfortably. Horses are very astute when it comes to people. We can spot tiny changes in a person's posture or voice. We know when they are tense, angry, or afraid. Robbie seemed very anxious about something. He soon left, his head slightly bowed in deep thought.

From that point on, Robbie was only sometimes his quietly chatty self. At other times, his attention seemed to be elsewhere. He would stare at the ground, fidgeting or quietly rocking, as if to calm himself.

Horses have lives that are largely independent of their human families. The majority of our days were spent grazing, dozing in the sun, and exploring our world. We are happiest when we have a lush pasture and a close equine friend to share it with. Maggie and I were content, and our days were a smooth ebb and flow of routine and season.

Late one afternoon, Maggie and I grazed near the fence as the boys played in the yard. Their parents sat on the porch reading magazines and sipping cold drinks. The boys, pretending to be soldiers, fired imaginary rounds at each other from long sticks, interrupting the mock gun battle periodically to perform improvised martial arts moves amid shouts of "Hi-ya!" and "Doh!" They began to make contact. Maggie and I backed away uneasily as the play fighting became rougher.

The mock battle soon escalated into a brawl, with the two older boys ganging up on Robbie. The smallest child struggled and protested, but by now they were no longer playing, and the excited shouts and squeals of laughter turned into panting, grunting, and Robbie's cries, as the boys landed blows in earnest. Robbie rolled into a tight ball, covering his head with his hands in a futile effort to protect himself. Helen looked anxiously on, glancing sideways at her husband.

Finally, Dan looked up from his magazine and yelled, "You boys cut it out! Stop it, Robbie!"

He shook his head slightly, as if in disappointment. "Time to grow up, boy." He went back to his magazine.

The two older boys got up and dusted themselves off, snickering and muttering insults in the direction of their youngest brother. As the two parents went back to their reading, the boys retrieved their sticks and wandered over to the fence, furtively poking each other. No one noticed Robbie quietly picking himself up and walking into the house.

Suddenly, Helen's voice rang out in a combination of disbelief and shock.

"Robbie! For God's sake, what are you doing?!"

Standing silently in the doorway, Robbie leaned his small body awkwardly against the frame. In his hands was his father's large black revolver. With an eerie, expressionless focus, Robbie held the gun out with both hands, aiming it unsteadily at his brothers, who were now motionless with fear. He pointed the barrel first at one, then the other.

Things happened very quickly after that. Dan lunged toward his son, as a sudden Pop! rang out. The older boys bolted for cover. Robbie, his slight body thrown backward by the recoil of the revolver, fell halfway through the door. The revolver clattered loudly onto the porch deck. Maggie and I sprang back, startled by the noise and confusion. We trotted off a few steps and then turned to look.

"Oh, no! No!" Helen stood seemingly paralyzed, her hands pressed over her mouth.

Dan leapt forward and grabbed the revolver from the floorboards. As he did, a patch of crimson appeared on his sleeve.

"You've been shot!" Helen said faintly, still in shock.

Dan inspected his arm briefly. "Just grazed, nothing to worry about."

Both parents' attention went quickly to the small boy lying in the doorframe. His mother bent over to help him up, sliding her arm under his shoulders to support him. Her face was ashen and uncomprehending. As she raised him slowly, she and Dan crouched lower to look closely at Robbie. "Robbie? Robbie!" Robbie seemed not to hear them. He appeared to be miles away, listening to the voices that only he could hear.

Soon afterward, the family left the house. Helen held Robbie protectively as they walked, her husband slightly ahead in stunned silence. The boys followed. They climbed into the station wagon and drove away, more slowly than usual.

In the days and weeks that followed, the boys were unusually subdued. Helen continued to feed us in the mornings but seemed distracted. We could sometimes see that she had been crying. The two older boys rarely fed Maggie or me in the evenings. We still had some remaining pasture for grazing, but we knew that something important had changed. Robbie had disappeared. Everyone seemed to have forgotten about us. Maggie and I kept close to each other, sensing the sorrow and confusion that had enveloped our family. Even Rufus stayed close, abandoning his usual pursuits, instead lying with quiet attention on the porch.

The day was overcast and still. Maggie and I stood side-by-side, swishing our tails, flicking away the occasional flies and listening to the distant trill of locusts. To that sound was added a far-off creaking, which grew slowly in volume. Soon, we could make out the bouncing shape of a pickup truck, carefully navigating the driveway's deep ruts.

Its driver was slender and wiry, dressed in a denim shirt, old blue jeans, and a scarlet baseball cap embroidered "UM." Helen walked out to greet him and they spoke softly, occasionally looking in our direction. We watched as they approached the fence.

"Mind if I hop on him?" the stranger asked.

"Not at all," Helen replied as she went to retrieve a bridle.

Her visitor inspected me carefully and picked up my feet. With the bit in my mouth, I stood still as the man effortlessly slid onto my back. He was balanced and knowledgeable, and I knew he had spent a lot of time on horseback. Bareback, he walked me around the pasture, and then we trotted a little. Maggie cheerfully bounced along beside us, hoping for a good game of chase.

"Yes, Ma'am," he said. "He'll do just fine. But I have no use for the miniature. I can ask around, if you'd like."

My heart stood still, and a rush of sadness came over me. I was to lose my second home, and worse, my sweet Maggie.

Helen nodded and sighed. "My youngest son was the only one who really cared about these ponies." She started to say more but stopped.

We left several hours later. The large trailer creaked and thumped as we started down the driveway. Alone in its dark interior, I worked to keep my balance as the wheels rolled over ruts and potholes. A hay net in the corner swished noisily to and fro. Over the sounds of the truck and the trailer, I heard Maggie frantically whinnying and racing along the fence line, trying her hardest to follow. I could hear her calling me for a long time, long after we were out of earshot.

Chapter 5

The Shadow Closes In

When the trailer finally pulled to a stop, I could smell other horses. Lots of them. I heard their excited whinnies as we drove up the driveway and they raced to the fence. They knew that horses often arrived on the trailer and were intensely curious.

The ranch lay at the base of the foothills. The small farmhouse was surrounded by a dozen pens and paddocks, most containing horses, nearly all of whom strained to get a look at me. A large wooden barn was located nearby.

As we walked past the paddocks, a couple of horses snapped at me, while others stood and stared with bold curiosity. A few had gone back to eating their hay and ignored me completely. We entered an empty corral, and the man unsnapped my lead and closed the gate. A small pile of hay, a shallow tub, and a tank of water were the corral's only features. Any grass had disappeared long ago.

I spent the long night eating the hay and listening to the sound of the large bodies around me, as they occasionally stirred and snorted in the darkness. I was worried and missed Maggie. In the midst of many horses, I felt very much alone.

Early the next morning, the man with the ball cap appeared with a second man. They began breaking bales of hay and spreading them in the paddocks and poured scoops of grain into small tubs in each. They added water to the troughs and removed manure that had accumulated overnight. I felt less anxious after eating my grain. There was food, other horses, and someone to take care of me. The men finished these chores in about two hours and then came back to my small corral.

"I thought he'd be a good size for the kids. He's sensible and quiet, and he's got good ground manners," said the man, whose name was Skeeter.

Earl, the other man, nodded. "Looks like a strong little feller. I get to name this one, right?"

Skeeter considered the question. "Yes sir, I believe it is your turn."

Earl thought for a moment. "I'm going to call him Sam."

Skeeter nodded. "Good enough."

The men got to work. They moved through the corrals, picked out individual horses, and led them to the barn, one by one.

After a brief but competent grooming, they fitted each with a bridle, blanket, and saddle, leaving the halter on under the bridle. They tied each horse to a long hitching post by the lead and halter, lining them up side by side until most were tacked up.

Shortly after that, the first cars began to arrive. They carried children and adults of all sizes and ages. They pulled up to the gravel lot beside the farmhouse, and the sound of low, excited voices filled the air. A small boy sounded out the words, "Crooked Ridge Stable, Hamilton, Montana."

Skeeter and Earl questioned each person briefly, pointing out particular horses. When all had arrived, the men escorted each person to a horse and helped them mount.

I watched the proceedings from my corral and was certain they had forgotten all about me, as few horses were left in the paddocks. But as the last riders prepared, Earl turned and pointed at me: "Skeet, let's take that little Appy."

"Young lady," Skeeter asked one of the arrivals, "Have you ever been on a horse? Only a little? Okay, see that little gray, spotted guy over there on the end? He's going to be your horse today. His name is Sam."

Skeeter brought me to the barn. He ran a brush over me quickly, picked my hooves, and selected a bridle and saddle from the racks of tack. He looked at the bridle, frowned slightly, and then adjusted the headstall smaller until it fit my head. In short order he added a blanket and a saddle. He motioned to a small figure behind me, and a young girl in tennis shoes and shorts approached slowly. He helped her into the saddle and handed her the reins.

"Honey, if you start to lose your balance, you just hold on to this horn, okay?"

By that time, the other horses were lining up behind Earl's, and Skeeter led me and my new charge over to stand behind a big Palomino, who stood with his young rider in resigned silence. I could feel the girl tentatively shift her weight. I raised my shoulder slightly to help her balance herself. "Hi, Sam," she said timidly.

"Okay, listen up everyone!" Earl shouted. "We are going to walk. No racing. No cowboy stuff. No taking off on your own. No riding up each other's butts. Keep your hands on your reins, keep your eyes open, and most of all, relax!" The group chuckled at the joke, and Earl and his horse stepped out.

The horses filed out behind him. They had done this every day and knew the route by heart. Reaching the end of the row of paddocks, we picked up a trail that wound up and around through the foothills. I followed the other horses, who knew where they were going, as my charge hung on tightly, clasping the horn whenever we came to a steep incline.

We followed the well-worn trail for several hours. I had not had much exercise in the last few years, and even with such a small rider, I was tired and sweating when we finally arrived back at the ranch.

The people dismounted, some with obvious pride in their accomplishment, others looking stiff and shaky, not used to being in a saddle for so long. My young charge was helped down, and she paused to gently pat my neck before I was led away. "Bye, Sam." We were all untacked and taken back to our pens. I took a long drink of water. I was sweaty and itchy, and it felt good to roll in the dirt and scratch my back. I stood up and shook myself off, dust swirling in the air around me.

We followed this same routine every day, missing days only when it rained. Sometimes, I had gentle riders, like my first charge, who were inexperienced but kind, while at other times I had more practiced children who could balance well and made my job easier. The worst were the little boys who liked to play rough when no one was watching. They would sometimes kick me in the sides or slap my neck with the reins to make me trot, before Earl or Skeeter could catch them and tell them to stop. Fearful riders sometimes kept the reins very tight, digging the bit into my mouth. Eventually, I learned to just appreciate the gentle riders and endure the bad—and to be relieved when we arrived back at the barn.

I gradually came to know the other horses. Some were friendly and calmly accepted my presence. Others flattened their ears and snapped in my direction to warn me away. A few kicked at me if I followed too closely. Most were simply resigned to their task, looking neither left nor right, performing their jobs with dull acceptance. I generally kept to myself, though I sometimes liked to visit with the friendlier horses on the trail. The big Palomino that I first noticed seemed especially kind. He was a gentle old guy who would walk beside me in relaxed companionship, a little stiff with arthritis.

Earl and Skeeter were businessmen. They knew that for us to do our jobs, we had to be fed. They never gave us more than we needed to eat or drink, but it was always just enough. However, their commercial outlook had a less fortunate side. If a horse injured itself or had other problems, it could be taken away and sold at any time. These were not sentimental people.

Summer turned to fall. Leaves blew across our paddocks like small, brightly colored butterflies. The number of tourists and riders slowed to a trickle. Those that arrived were bundled in coats and gloves, and they often rode hunched down against the wind. Meanwhile, we grew our own winter apparel, and our sleek coats were replaced by longer, thicker coats that protected us from the cold. Though I continued to carry children on the trails, more and more horses remained behind. Finally, the riders stopped coming entirely, and we spent our days in the paddocks.

Under a hazy, white sky with the tinny smell of winter in the air, I watched Earl and Skeeter begin to load up horses in the large stock trailer. They selected them from the paddocks and led them in one at a time. The last of these was the gentle, old Palomino. He turned briefly to look at the ranch one last time before stepping stiffly into the trailer and disappearing through the back door. Earl and Skeeter closed the trailer doors and drove away, leaving only a handful of us among the many empty paddocks.

Those of us that remained were turned out into the field, where we stayed over the winter. We did no more trail riding for months. The following spring, we were brought back to the paddocks and watched as new horses arrived, one or more at a time. The pattern continued. Horses came and left every year, but I always remained, wintering over along with a small group of horses.

It was during the first winter that I awoke early one morning with a pain in my eyes. They stung and ached as if there was something in them. Tears flowed down my cheeks. By the next day, I felt better and soon forgot about it. But it happened again, then again. Bright sun and wind sometimes made them hurt so badly that I had to clench them shut. Other days, they bothered me very little. Eventually, my eyes hurt more often than not.

In addition to the pain, I began to have trouble seeing at night. I once had excellent night vision. Now, everything after dusk melted into a dark blur. I could see large objects and knew where I was, but I could not always make out fence lines and occasionally tripped over a bucket or tub not in its usual place. For a while, I could still see well during the day, but then I began to lose my vision even in bright light.

Still, I knew the farm and trail so well that I really didn't depend on my vision. I knew every twist and slope of the rocky foothills. And I was walking with other horses who also knew their way. But as I began to have trouble seeing smaller objects, I stumbled over rocks and sticks, causing my riders to tense up and grab the saddle horn.

One day, returning to the ranch down a rocky incline, I tripped over a fallen sapling I was unable to see. Trying to regain my balance, I lurched forward to steady myself. In the process, I nearly unseated my rider, a young woman with very little experience. Startled, she grabbed the horn and let out a shout as I stumbled forward, passing the horse to my right. The stones I dislodged rolled down the slope ahead of me, causing the horses in front of me to turn and shy. Finally, everyone regained their composure and assumed their previous positions, with the exception of my rider, who clung desperately to the saddle horn for the remainder of the ride.

The incident was not lost on Earl and Skeeter. That evening, after we had come back from the trail, I heard them talking in low tones as they leaned against the fence.

"Looks like Sam might be going blind," Skeeter admitted reluctantly. He leaned over the rail, his eyes lowered as if paying close attention to a rock or bug.

"I've been watching that. It's a pity," sighed Earl. "He's been a good one. I sure hate to send him to the auction, though. I kind of like the little guy. But we can't risk having him fall and hurt someone."

"Who's going to want him?" Skeeter asked. He examined a small pebble with the toe of his boot, contemplating the answer. "He isn't worth much."

"I don't know." Earl shrugged. "He can still see some. Harley's got some grandkids. He might want this pony."

Skeeter nodded. "Hmm. Okay, then."

Chapter 6

Freedom Gained, Freedom Lost

We left for Harley's some days later. This time, it was only me in the stock trailer. I no longer had a best friend to say goodbye to, or any fondness for the ranch, Earl, or Skeeter. I didn't know where I was going, but there had always been someone to take care of me, and there had always been food.

When we arrived at Harley's ranch, I could not detect any other horses. The air was cool and clear, and I could smell water. Harley came out to meet us and walked to the back of the trailer. Moving slowly and a little stooped, he seemed old, his silver hair infused with the aroma of tobacco. He led me into a small pen attached to a barn overhang. He filled the tank with water, and I took a long drink.

"Well, hi there, fella," he whispered in a soft, slightly trembling voice. He reached over and scratched my neck.

There was little grass in the pen but plenty of hay to eat. I spent the next few days there, adjusting to my new surroundings.

I knew that there were pastures around us, and that there were cows in them. I could not see very far, but I could smell them. I knew something about cows, as I had met them when I was young. I never truly understood them, but they seemed generally friendly, if a little shy.

Several days later, Harley led me through the small gate and released me into the field. "Okay, Bub. You go on out and meet the neighbors," he encouraged.

I began to orient myself in the large meadow. First, I smelled for other horses, and then I checked for dangerous animals. Sensing neither, I located the fence line and began to walk. It seemed to be miles long. For a while, I simply walked, listening to the birds and stopping occasionally to graze. It was a bright, clear day, and while I remained alert and cautious, it was a pleasant environment.

Ultimately, I sensed that I was approaching a herd of cattle. Their dark, shadowy forms soon appeared on the banks of a stream that ran beneath the fence. I had never seen this many cattle in one place. Their sturdy black bodies extended as far as I could see, blending into one large, black mass that covered the ground for miles, or so it seemed.

I slowed to a stop and waited politely while they inspected me. A few cows exhaled sharply or shook their heads in warning. But most just continued to stare at me, chewing their cuds. I began to graze, watching them out of one eye in case I needed to run away quickly. But most of them soon lost interest and began to ignore me.

My new home was enormous. In contrast to the small pens I knew well, the pastures stretched for miles, over which the herd of cattle roamed. The fields were green and lush. The rushing stream provided plenty of cool water, and there were enough trees for ample shade.

As the cattle became more comfortable with me, I began to blend in with the herd, gradually moving closer to them for companionship and protection. They were, in fact, surprisingly good company—gentle and sensible, but fierce if threatened.

If something frightened me, I knew to run away as quickly as I could. I had learned that as a foal. But cattle often stand and face the source of their fear, and they can inflict serious injury on an attacker. I sometimes saw wolves slink around the edges of the herd, eyeing the calves but keeping a careful distance from the cows, who lowered their heads and pawed. Wolves are usually no match for adult cattle. Even mountain lions limit their predation to the sick or injured.

Over time, I noticed that the same cattle tended to graze near me. Previously, all cattle simply smelled like cattle. But I came to realize that they had smells as unique as horses, and I began to recognize individuals. As we grazed, we moved slowly along, step by step, nearly in unison. At night, while I slept stretched out flat, my companions rested upright on their chests, quietly chewing their cuds next to me in comfortable silence. We became friends.

One of my companions was a huge, older cow who appeared to be in charge of everyone around her. The other was a lively young heifer who always wanted to play with me. At first, she startled me by reaching over and running her huge, rough tongue across my neck in a juicy display of bovine affection. When I jumped back, she jumped too, hoping that I was ready to play. Wherever I went, these two were never far behind.

I enjoyed the freedom of this life. No one ever asked me to do anything. I did not carry riders over the same, rocky trail. I could eat green grass and drink from clear streams, and, at the end of the day, find a soft place to sleep. The herd's large size meant that there were many eyes to detect predators, so I could relax at night. During the day, I often dozed in the sunshine, my herd grazing around me.

In winter, the wind whistled through the valley, and snow blew into deep drifts. But we found shelter under trees, and I stayed warm among the large herd. There was still plenty of grass underneath the snow. As spring arrived, the snow melted, and bright, new grass appeared. New calves arrived, too, as tiny and fragile as fawns.

My eyes were my only problem. They still burned and ached on some days. I could not see anything at night, and during the day most objects were blurry. But I had become accustomed to my loss of vision. I always knew where I was and had keen senses of hearing and smell. I rarely stumbled in the expansive pasture and had the constant company of my cattle friends to alert me to danger.

I was in fact, as happy as I had been in many years.

But the world is an uncertain place. And by then, I had come to realize that change is the nature of things. This life would change, too.

We first heard them in the early morning, low voices that carried a long distance in the chill air. And then I could smell horses. This was very exciting to me because I knew that my herd would be better with other horses in it. However, that was not to be the case.

As riders got closer, I heard the sounds of whistles and whips. The cattle closest to the sounds were unnerved by the sudden appearance of men on horseback, and they moved away from them. The entire herd reacted in near unison, and soon we all moved away, my herd mates lowing and bawling as I was carried along in a current of a thousand large bodies.

We headed toward the ranch, a long line of dark shapes that stretched to the horizon as one dark stream. As we approached, we met other riders on horseback who moved in from the sides and directed us into a large paddock. The horsemen closed the gate behind us, and my herd milled around anxiously, unsure of what to do.

As the cattle began to calm down, I heard the men talking, and I moved a little closer to listen.

"Shame about Harley."

"I think he held on as long as he could."

"Is Sue Anne managing the sale?"

Throughout the day, the men worked in the adjacent field. I heard the sounds of shouts and clanging as they set up large metal panels. I also heard the unmistakable creaking of large stock trailers and the smell of diesel. We were tired, frightened, hungry, and thirsty. I had lost my friends, with no hope of finding them in the chaos.

Early the next morning, the men began to drive the cattle out in groups through the gate of the paddock. The riders isolated a group from the herd, driving them from behind and through the opening. The animals entered a chute that had been constructed using the metal panels. The chute then led them into the trailers. I could hear the thumping and bouncing of cattle feet as the animals milled around inside, then the clanging of the doors as they shut. Each trailer drove away and was replaced immediately by another, which promptly backed up to the chute.

The herd in the paddock became progressively smaller. Like my herd mates, I shied away from the herders' whistles and cracks. The horsemen unnerved me, and I tried to avoid them by hiding behind my herd mates, as I was no taller than they were.

But one of the riders spotted me and turned in my direction. I backed away, trying to disappear among the cattle. Just as I thought I had succeeded, I felt the weight of a stiff rope settling around my neck. I jumped sideways in fear, and the rope tightened. No matter how hard I struggled, I could not escape it. I reared and fought but could not get away. I was trapped.

Finally, I stood frozen with fear, the rope taut between the horseman and me. He wrapped the rope around the saddle horn to secure it. His horse backed up, keeping the tension between us. The cattle moved away, and I was left alone to face my captor.

The man dismounted, holding the end of the rope. He began to speak, moving toward me slowly.

"You're okay, buddy. You just calm down, now." His voice was quiet and measured.

As he got closer, I could see that he wore a denim jacket and cowboy hat. He was a tanned, older man but moved with the strength and energy of a much younger person. He smelled of coffee and smoke.

I tried to back away, but in his voice I heard the sound of a friend, not a predator. I stopped and listened, still wary, but beginning to understand that he meant no harm. When he finally reached me, he slowly raised his hand to my brow, gently rubbing my face in a way that no one had in a long time. I breathed a deep sigh and began to relax.

With the rope still around my neck, I walked with the man and his horse in the direction of the ranch house. We exited the far side of the paddock, where a couple of men leaned against the fence, watching us.

"What was he doing in there?"

"I heard Harley got him for the grandkids, but they never got to see him."

"Well if no one else wants him, I guess I could take him for Darla's little girl."

"Go on, then."

Chapter 7

William

"Dad, what on earth were you thinking?" Darla stood with her hands on her hips, irritation rising in her voice. She seemed a big woman, with things that sparkled and jangled hanging from her wrists.

"I just thought that Sissy might like a pony. Look, he's pretty friendly." There was the hint of an apology in his voice.

"And exactly who is going to take care of him? She's only four! She could get kicked or stepped on for Pete's sake. She doesn't even know how to ride." Darla seemed to bite the words off invisible sentences and hurl them at her father.

The man let out a deep sigh. "She could learn. He's got some age to him, and these older fellas can make the best teachers. How about we keep him at my place, and I can teach her when she comes to visit?"

So, I went to live with this man named Bob, father to the

imperious Darla and grandfather to little Sissy. I moved into a small dirt pen behind a house. The pen had once served as a chicken run. The coop was still there, though Bob had attached a small overhang that served partly to keep his tools and equipment out of the rain. Now, it also served as shelter for me, as well as the pen's current inhabitant, a small brown and white goat.

"Here you go, William," Bob told the goat. "Company!"

"Eeeeeeh!" The unearthly scream stopped me in my tracks. It was the sound of a wounded animal suffering excruciating pain. But Bob cheerfully urged me forward. Reluctantly, I went.

As soon as I stepped through the gate, I could feel the small body trotting around me in circles, and I was nearly overwhelmed by the pungent, acrid smell of this unfamiliar animal. I shied away but could not seem to escape the curious little creature that followed me everywhere, even as I kept bumping into the wire sides of the enclosure that I could not see.

Despite his long time alone in this dreary pen and his terrifying bleat, William was a gentle soul who appeared delighted by my presence. He sniffed me and tugged at my tail and seemed to be everywhere at once. Recognizing that I could not escape him, I settled down for my own investigation, moving in to get a closer look.

I could just make out the smooth-haired little body with large dark patches and enormous ears. A pair of ivory-colored horns curled backward on his head. Aside from his horrible body odor, he was a good-natured guy with a tail that flicked in constant amusement.

I had learned to live with cattle, and now my only herd mate was a goat. This was not awful in itself, as we are both herd animals and preferred to have each other's company over none at all. William was thrilled with this new arrangement, making every effort to welcome me with his best goat manners. But even a pretty good herd mate can sometimes be annoying, and William had his quirks.

It seemed his sole ambition to climb up onto my back. Sometimes, while dozing in the sun, I felt the sudden sharp pressure of two small hooves pushing against my side, as if he was testing it. I would step away quickly, and William would delicately hop down, nonchalantly pretending to be engaged in something else.

But he got bolder. Sometimes, he added a slight hop to this effort, causing me to flinch in discomfort. More disturbingly, he sometimes came up quietly behind me and gave a quick tug to my tail, which was becoming progressively shorter. William was, in fact, slowly eating it.

Bob came out every day to top the water trough and bring us hay and feed, the latter of which William sometimes stole from me if Bob wasn't paying attention. Bob was gentle and quiet.

He had a genuine fondness for William and clearly understood horses. He would reach over and scratch that wonderful spot on my withers, and I learned to trust him.

Still, he spent little time with us. The pen was muddy and unpleasant and smelled of damp feathers from long-ago chickens. William and I often strained to reach through the wire fence for blades of fresh grass; we were not very successful. I found myself longing for the large, grassy meadow and my cattle friends.

The faint smell of wood smoke and cooking food wafted from the small house. As William and I munched on the remnants of the morning's hay, a car pulled up and parked on the side of the house. Its occupants included Darla, a man, and a small girl.

As the trio approached the house, Darla held the little girl protectively by the hand. "Now don't you go gettin' those new shoes dirty," she warned. Bob greeted them warmly, and they entered the house. We could hear the sounds of the family inside, voices rising and falling, dishes clattering.

"How's that no-account cousin of yours? Arrested yet?"

"Now, Dad…," a voice started, before breaking off in muffled laughter.

"I never did understand libertarians," came another voice, emphatically making a point.

"And how's your momma's health these days?"

The friendly chatter continued throughout the afternoon. Meanwhile, William and I munched on our hay and dozed in the sun, only occasionally picking up our ears at an interesting noise or twitching when a fly landed on us.

"Sissy, you want to come see that pony I got you? His name is Chico."

Darla's voice rose and tightened in response.

"Now, Dad, I thought we'd discussed this. Sissy will not have a pony. She is too young, and I will not have her coming back home covered in mud and horse crap." The two voices continued in low argument, her voice biting, his softly pleading, but in the end the family said their goodbyes and left without visiting us.

The next day, something very unexpected happened. I was standing near the corner of the pen, snoozing in the sun and listening to far-away sounds. I now relied on my hearing more than ever, and my world had become one of bird calls, animal noises, distant cars, and voices and sounds I could not identify. But I should have been paying more attention to the sounds inside the pen.

Suddenly, I was knocked nearly sideways by the impact of William's hooves, striking one side of my back first, then the other in quick succession. The clever goat had been pondering the problem of how to jump up on my back and had finally calculated that he could do so with a running jump.

However, he had not considered two things. First, because goats do not excel at physics, he did not anticipate that his momentum might prevent him from stopping once he'd reached his target. Second, I was a pony with limited vision, and he failed to consider that I might react badly to such a surprise.

William could not, in fact, stop. He continued forward, stumbling across my back and straight over the top of the wire enclosure. At the same time, I was jolted awake and panicked, thinking I was under attack by a predator I could not see. I bolted forward, crashing into the wire fence. It had been sufficient to hold chickens but could not restrain a pony in full flight. The wire stretched and crumpled, the old posts snapping as the fence gave way.

Hearing the ruckus, Bob rushed outside to find William prancing proudly around the yard, me trotting around frightened, snorting, and totally disoriented, and the ruins of the pen's wire fence in an unrepairable tangle.

He let out a low groan. "What in creation?"

William and I spent the night tied to the remaining posts of the demolished fence. The next day, a truck with a small horse trailer pulled up to the house.

Bob greeted its driver, a big, surly fellow who wasted little time with small talk.

"I just can't keep them. This pony is friendly, and if you can give him a good home, I'd be much obliged."

The man nodded and grunted. "Sure, we'll take him."

The man led me up the back of the trailer. I walked carefully, as I could no longer see the step and had to proceed cautiously. On the way out of the driveway, we passed another truck pulling a small trailer. It appeared that at long last, the clever William would be out of that pen for good. I did not know where I was going, but I was happy for him.

Chapter 8

The Sound of Fear

The trailer lurched and creaked as we rolled down the long driveway, navigating its dips and ruts. More than once, I was thrown into its side.

By now, I could see very little that was not near my face, or in bright light. Most of the world appeared to me in shades of blue, green, and brown that all blended together without form. I could still avoid walking into large objects but could not see anything small. At night, I could see virtually nothing.

My sense of hearing was still very acute, and I could hear even tiny sounds that most people missed. I could feel the wind at my face, and my sense of smell told me much about my surroundings. I could find food and water easily, simply by smell. And I always knew where I was in the world because of my excellent sense of navigation. But I needed to memorize the locations of fence lines because they were very hard to see, and to walk carefully to avoid stumbling over rocks and stumps. Overhanging branches were a particular hazard.

I had also become progressively stiffer in the mornings, especially during cold weather. I had always been a strong, stout pony. But I no longer moved with the effortless grace of a young horse. I was, in fact, getting quite old. Sometimes, it took effort to stand up.

Once we arrived at our destination, I was led across the uneven ground until I heard the sound of a gate unlatching. We walked through it, and my halter and lead were removed. With my limited vision, I had to investigate this new territory carefully.

"Where'd you get him, Dad?"

"What's his name? Oh! I want to give him a name!"

"Can we pet him?"

The enthusiastic young voices seemed to come from the direction of the fence we had just come through. Questions were asked more quickly than they could be answered.

"How about Snowball?"

"No! I got it! Speedy!" The voices giggled.

"Can I give him a carrot?

"Shh! I think his name should be Tony Pony!" the smallest voice pronounced grandly.

I was in some kind of paddock located in a clearing and surrounded, apparently, by woods. I surmised the latter because woods have an earthy, green smell of bark and damp moss. Later, the sounds of crickets and katydids confirmed this. After circling my enclosure cautiously to get my bearings, I went over to the fence to meet the children.

A small hand appeared on my nose, petting it gently. It was soon joined by other hands that rubbed my cheeks and neck. I stood there with my nose stretched out, enjoying these soft caresses. I counted three hands. Two belonged to a pair of girls. The smallest hand, still busy petting my nose, belonged to a little boy. Adult voices spoke in the background.

"Okay, so you happy now?" the man who brought me there asked. There was something unpleasant in his voice that I couldn't quite identify. And he had an unusual odor about him. It smelled a little like the beer that Earl and Skeeter sometimes drank in the evenings, after the horses had been put up.

A woman sighed. "I know Bob appreciated us taking him. The kids and me'll feed and water him. He won't be any trouble."

The man grunted. "You make sure he isn't. Too many mouths to feed around here as it is." He turned to leave, walking away heavily and, from the sound, a little unsteadily. The woman let out a long breath and with a sudden forced cheerfulness said, "Okay, everyone! What's his name gonna' be?"

Ultimately, I was christened "Super Fast Lightening," shortened later to "Lightening." I had nothing more for shelter in the paddock than a small run-in shed. I discovered that it was not a large paddock and was mostly full of weeds. But the children and their mother made sure I had fresh hay and water every day, as well as a scoop full of soft, pelleted grain. This was far easier for me to eat than the hay, which I couldn't chew very well any more. Horses don't get cavities, but as we age, we begin to lose some of our teeth, making it difficult to chew any but soft food.

In the afternoons, the family walked down the short trail, through the trees to the paddock. I could hear the sounds of conversation in the distance, the smaller voices occasionally piping in with important proclamations. They brought with them a small, plastic basket of grooming supplies, and the children took turns brushing my body, mane, and tail. Sarah, the mom, would sometimes bring me peppermints or lemon cookies, which I loved.

These were good days. Sarah and her children were affectionate and kind. Every so often, the children's father accompanied them on their routine. He usually talked to Sarah while my young friends fed me and gave me a good going-over. Most days, he joked with the children or discussed other matters with his wife, sometimes reaching over to give my neck a rub. But on other days, he was different.

Then, I could smell the peculiar odor on him that I'd first noticed, and his voice sounded different, somehow slower and more exaggerated. There was a suspicious edge to it, as if he was secretly angry and waiting for an opportunity to strike out. Those days, he generally found one. Whether it was something Sarah said or an excuse to discipline the kids, some child usually ended up crying. Sarah sometimes tried gently to intervene, but the menace in his voice was unmistakable, and I knew that at those times, she feared him. The mood became quiet and subdued, and the family did not stay for long.

I spent my days munching on the hay and grain they brought me, listening to the sounds of the creatures in the woods that surrounded us, and napping in the sun. I had no animal companions, but my family helped fill this void. Every day, I waited for them by the fence, my ears alert for the sounds of the children as they came out with their basket and treats. They were unfailing in their attention. As the seasons passed and fall became winter, the children still came. Even during the coldest weather, they piled out, bundled in warm coats, grooming my long hair with mittened hands. During summer months, they spent longer periods with me, talking or sometimes just sitting with me in the evening sun.

Over time, the father accompanied them less and less. When he did, he was unpleasant and intimidating, and he more often had that peculiar odor.

"Momma, what's wrong?" The approaching voices asked cautiously one day. "Did you hurt yourself?"

"Nuthin', you. Did you remember to bring the peppermints?"

The children were unusually quiet as they finished their evening routine. The youngest child stood close to me, his ear tight to my side as if listening to my heart, his hand slowly rubbing circles on my belly.

The next day, things were back to normal, though Sarah was still reserved.

The family continued to spend every evening with me, making sure I was fed and well cared for, but a new caution entered the voices of even the children, who were just a little more subdued and a little slower to laugh. Something was wrong. The youngest boy continued to hold himself close to me, as if trying to disappear in my now white coat.

"What're you lookin' at, you big shaggy-ass mutt?" Their father's growl seemed to hesitate at every syllable, apparently for emphasis. The children silently brushed my coat. Sarah said nothing.

"Here you go, then! Run!" A small projectile bounced off my neck, landing on the ground with a metallic "plink." I flinched, startled and confused, as the shiny object rolled away from us. The children stiffened in alarm.

"Now Trey, that pony hasn't done anything to you." Sarah tried to be nonchalant, but I could hear the tightness in her voice.

"No, he just takes up your every, stinkin', waking hour. Every single day you waste your time fooling with this raggedy old goat, instead of fixing me a decent meal once in a while. You think I'd see some appreciation after I've spent all day trying to provide for your worthless hides...."

To the slurring voice was added a note of self-pity. "I tell you what. We were better off without this little piece of horsemeat. But we can fix that real quick. Yes, Sir." The children, it seemed, didn't dare to breathe.

"Come on, Trey. It's getting late. Let's get back and I'll make us all a nice supper," Sarah pleaded softly.

I felt a sharp pain as another small object, possibly a stone, glanced off my shoulder. I flinched again.

"Made you move, you little jackass."

"Please, Trey, let's just go."

"You shut up, or I'll give you something to worry about! Just who do you think you are? Kids, your mother here seems to be getting a bit big for her britches, don't you think? Sounds like she needs another lesson in good manners!"

The slurred speech had become a menacing growl, and Trey now seemed to be spitting out every word. No one else dared speak.

"Hah! Come on then, you bunch of ingrates! After you, Your Majesty. I'll deal with you later."

The family quickly and silently picked up the grooming items. Within moments, they were gone.

I just stood there, confused and unsettled. In my entire life, no one had ever lifted a hand toward me. Even the stupid little boys on the trail rides had always stopped short of doing anything abusive, thanks partly to the watchful eyes of Skeeter and Earl. People were always kind to me. I simply did not understand.

The following evening, I waited patiently for my family. But they never came. As the night closed in, I wandered off to nibble a few strands of grass poking through the stock-wire fence, trying out several of the weeds, just in case they were edible. There was still water in the tank, but I was concerned. Where was my family? I spent the evening picking among strands of old hay scattered on the ground.

A large, soft object swished by my head and hit the ground with a dull thump. "Here you go, you worthless piece of shoe leather!" Trey had thrown a half bale of hay into the paddock, and I was happy to see it. I had endured three days without being fed. I heard the sound of water filling the trough. I drank anxiously, wary of Trey and still listening for my family. But he soon left. I never saw Sarah or the children again.

From that time on, I never knew whether I would be fed. Some days, a half bale of hay sailed over the fence; on other days, no one came to give me hay or even water. The soft grain had disappeared, and I could swallow only small bits of hay because of my bad teeth.

Trey had that peculiar odor about him all the time. Though desperate for food, I often stood away from him because I never knew when he would throw something at me or lash out. Most of the time, the objects he threw went wild because his aim wasn't very good. But I could not see well enough to get out of the way, and sometimes the stones and rocks hit me hard, and I would grunt in pain.

I had never known hunger or cruelty. I had always had green pastures to graze in or people who brought me grain and hay. But now, there was a deep, ever-present gnawing in my stomach. I worried constantly. Would there be food? Who would take care of me? Where were my people? I kept searching the paddock ground for any leftover hay. I listened for the sound of approaching footsteps but often heard none for days.

Months passed, and every day I worried about food and water. The hunger continued until my stomach ached. I grew thinner. My once soft coat now hung from my sides in dirty clumps. When I lay down to sleep on the cold ground, it became harder and harder to get up.

When I finally heard footsteps approaching, I let out a whinny of relief and desperation. I was so hungry that I was willing to face anything, as long as I had something to eat.

"Ah, Geez." It was not Trey's voice. It was the voice of a younger man. As he approached the fence, I came up eagerly to find out if he had anything to eat.

"You poor old guy. What on earth…?" The question was left unfinished. The man filled my trough, and while I gulped down the water, he gathered up the old hay that had fallen on the ground outside the pen.

"Best I can do for you, Pal. Just hang on."

Hours later, the man came back, accompanied by Trey. As they walked toward the pen, I could hear them talking.

"Now, Trey, you know I don't want to get all in your business, but the law says you need to feed and water your animals. This horse is very thin, and you're going to have to feed him better. That means grain, not just hay. He's an old guy, and his teeth aren't up to this. You need to keep that trough filled, too."

"He isn't mine, and she can come back here and get him any time she wants. She could have come out here herself, if she gave a good hoot."

"Nonetheless, he's on your property, and you are responsible for him until she does. Sorry about all this, man." He patted Trey on the shoulder. "I'll be back to check on him. You call me if you need anything."

As the man walked off, Trey stood by the side of the fence. When he was finally alone, he spoke slowly, glaring at me, his voice cold with rage.

"Oh, we'll fix this, you little dirt bag. Oh, yessiree we will."

‑‑‑‑‑‑‑

After that, I spent most of my time at the far end of the paddock. I was hungry, but I also wanted to keep a safe distance from Trey, who I thought might hurt me. I continued to hope for food but feared the person who might bring it.

The next time I heard Trey's voice, it was accompanied by the softer voice of a much older man. His steps were slower, and it appeared that he had difficulty navigating the short trail from the house to the paddock.

"I can't believe she called the Sheriff."

"Son, she's just worried about him, and I guess she didn't know what else to do. He sure isn't much to look at, is he?"

"I just want him gone, as soon as we can haul his mangy carcass out of here."

"Okay, okay. I'll put him in with Buster, just to keep the peace. He can probably use the company."

"Thanks, Pop."

When Trey came to get me, I shied away at first. He muttered briefly under his breath, but I sensed that this time, he was not going to hurt me, and I let him approach. He led me up the short track to the small trailer that brought me here. As we walked, I kept trying to sneak mouthfuls of grass that grew around the edge of the yard. I was so hungry, and the fresh green grass tasted like heaven. Trey jerked my head up as I tried to eat.

I was going to leave! I strode boldly into the trailer. I was ready to go.

Chapter 9

Hunger

This time, the journey was short. We arrived at Pop's house after traversing a number of back roads that caused the trailer to bounce and sway. When we arrived, I could smell another horse, as well as other animals. Having a horse for company was a welcome development.

I was eager to take in my new surroundings but could see very little. I smelled the air and listened to everything as I was taken to my new home. I was especially curious about my new herd mate, a gelding. As we entered the paddock, I could feel mud beneath my feet and knew that there would be little or no grass here. I hesitated, listening in all directions to locate my new herd mate.

I didn't need to wait for long. I could hear the sound of the horse moving toward me, each hoof pulling out of the mud with a soft sucking sound. He stopped a short distance away to examine me. I stood quietly and smelled the air. Finally, he approached. He smelled my breath and then let out a squeal and jump—I was in his yard, and he was the boss. I backed away a few steps to show that I understood. Having resolved the issue, I began to explore my surroundings.

There was little to take in. The paddock was low and swampy, but a small stream ran through it, and I was happy to see water. I took a long drink. The paddock was not large, and the only shelter was some type of building that seemed to be collapsing slowly, as the walls were inclined sideways. I needed to tread carefully so as not to trip on the loose boards scattered on the ground.

My new herd mate was named Buster. He was very quiet after our initial introduction; he did not seem very lively. I soon discovered the reason for this. Near the center of the paddock were the remains of a large, round bale of hay. I was so hungry that I eagerly searched the pile for edible strands, but most of it was moldy and ruined, with little food value. Even this poor food was better than nothing. But Buster was too weak to have much interest.

The paddock ground seemed permanently soggy. Small pools formed in the tracks of our hooves, and every step involved a slosh or sucking sound. Every so often, it dried out enough for Pop to bring the tractor in with a new bale of hay. On those days, Buster and I parked beside the bale, digging deep inside it with our noses, looking for edible hay. In my case, the strands had to be small and soft, as I could not chew the larger stalks. We worked on each bale for weeks, until rain caused it to soften and collapse. Soon after, the hay became muddy and dank with mold, and we slowly ran out of food. During those times, we foraged constantly to find enough to eat, waiting on a change in weather and the next bale.

We rarely saw Pop. Sometimes we heard him talking to himself in a soft voice as he made his way around the farm, tending to his cattle and other animals. Pop had a wife, and we could hear her moving about the chicken coop, collecting eggs. We heard the metal clanging of a can when she fed them. She never came down to the paddock.

Day after day, rain or shine, Buster and I searched for food among the remnants of the rotting, round bales. We ceased this activity only when the weather forced us to seek shelter in the old building, or when the hay was so badly ruined that there was no food to be found. Neither Buster nor I had much strength. When we were out of food, we could only stand and wait, hoping for drier weather and listening to the sounds of birds, cattle, or other animals. We were companions to each other's hunger and misery, but had energy for little else. The days stretched into months, and the months became seasons.

The sudden scolding of a Blue Jay alerted us to the visitors, and we heard approaching voices. One of them was Pop's; the second was dreaded and familiar.

"The horse auction starts at eight tomorrow morning, but I can run up to Missoula and drop them off there this evening." Trey's voice filled me with anxiety, and I was instantly on guard.

"While you're in town, would you mind picking me up a block of sulfur salt for the cows?"

Trey and Pop led us out of the paddock. We walked beside the two men, up the hill and into Trey's small trailer. The door of the trailer closed with a rusty creak, and I could hear Trey humming as he walked around to the driver's side of the truck. There was something unpleasant about the sound.

Chapter 10

The Loss of Almost Everything

When we pulled to a stop, Trey got out of the truck and disappeared. A cacophony of sounds and smells surrounded us. Men's voices argued and laughed. Engines rumbled. The pungent smell of gas and diesel smoke hung in the air. And animals thumped and banged as they shifted in their trailers. I smelled coffee and cooking food, as well as horses, cattle, goats, and other animals I did not recognize. I had never been to a place like this, and I struggled to understand what I was hearing. I had never wished to see so badly.

"Your pen is down near the end, behind the building," a man's voice said, and Trey started the truck.

After a few minutes, the trailer pulled around and stopped. I followed Buster as we were led along what seemed to be a narrow aisle between corrals, some containing anxious horses.

In the dim light, I could see very little, but I could hear them circling and snorting, and occasionally a nose reached through the bars of the metal pens as we passed. Our hooves clip-clopped across the concrete walkway. The smell was overwhelming, and the air was heavy with manure, the bodies of many animals, and fear. I could also make out a faint, putrid smell. There was death in this place, and I was afraid.

"Buh-bye, Horsemeat." I flinched as something crashed loudly against the metal bars. I heard Trey chuckle as he walked down the aisle, leaving us alone in the pen.

Frightened, I circled the enclosure to determine its dimensions and find a way out. I also tried not to run into Buster, who also paced anxiously. At times, I could hear other horses being led in and released into the pens near us.

The horses jostled and kicked at each other. I could hear thumping and clanging as submissive horses tried to get away from the more aggressive animals in the overcrowded pens. Elsewhere, we heard the occasional crash and thump of a panicked horse running up against the side of a pen, sometimes accompanied by the crack of a whip or a shouted curse. The pen beside us contained a horse that was strangely quiet, and I could smell the sickness about him. One horse that walked past us smelled faintly of blood, and I think he had been injured.

Amid all this was the steady rise and fall of voices as men talked and joked.

"I saw Hank over at Fallon last week. He was headed up north with another string of old riding stable horses."

"I've got a nice big paint colt here you might want to look at. It'd be a shame to sell him for meat."

"None of these are any good. They're either lame or wild. Guess they'll go up to Bouvrey. At least the prices are good at the moment."

As afternoon became evening, the remaining light faded. Fewer horses were brought in, and few people remained. Though the pens had quieted down, we could still hear the sounds of voices and country western music out in the parking lot. Occasionally, the silence in the pens was broken by the thump of a disturbed horse suddenly kicking out, followed by the jostling of the animals around him, until all settled down. Not many slept, and the air was thick with apprehension.

Buster and I had the pen to ourselves. We stood close together for comfort and protection in this dark place, ears alert. We spent the night watchful and waiting, not knowing what would happen. I was more afraid than I had ever been in my life.

The faint light told me it was early morning, and horses and people began to stir. Out in the parking lot, I heard a truck pull up and the sound of a door slamming and approaching voices. Soon, other vehicles began to arrive, and the smell of coffee wafted through the air. A man walked down the aisle, humming to himself and smelling of cigarettes. I heard him stop at one of the pens to check on the horses inside.

As the sky brightened, the sound of hooves clattered in the aisle; more horses were being brought in. Many more arrived than the day before, and the pens became so crowded that the horses constantly bumped and jostled each other. Occasionally, one would squeal or kick out. I was overwhelmed by the sounds and smells of frightened animals.

There were more people, too. They talked casually and joked about the horses they had brought in, their light conversation at odds with the fear of their horses. But there were other conversations, too. A few people walked through the aisle way and paused before each pen, looking through the metal poles to examine the occupants of each enclosure.

"That one's got a BLM brand. Mustang."

"Take a look at this big gelding over here. He's got shoes."

The voices paused in front of our pen. I wondered if the people might have food. We had not eaten since the evening before, and we had no water. Surely someone would help us. I pricked up my ears.

"Poor old guys. Who on earth is going to bid on those?" They moved on, and the hunger continued to gnaw at us.

Soon, we could hear the sound of many voices talking in the distance. There were more people than I had ever heard together in one place. Their voices blended into a loud hum, which grew in volume until a strange, echoing voice caused them to fall silent.

"Good morning ladies and gentlemen. We're going to start this morning with some Double T Ranch liquidation horses. All Quarter horses. First up, here's a nice big, gelding. He's eight years old and well broke. We're going to start him at twelve hundred, so who'll give me twelve?"

The auctioneer's voice rolled into a fast, singsong rhythm, occasionally punctuated by a rising number, as if asked as a question. Around him, people shouted: "Here! Here!" The auctioneer made note and moved on. The rhythm of his voice finally slowed.

"Seven twenty-five. Do I hear seven and a half? Seven and a half? Seven and a half? Sold! Seven twenty-five!" We heard a loud "Bang!" and the auctioneer ceased his chant.

"Gentleman over there, number 351. Good buy on that horse."

And so it went. One after another, horses were ridden into the auction pit. The auctioneer worked the crowd, sometimes jovial, sometimes pleading, sometimes lecturing.

"You all asleep out there? Nine hundred—you, over there! Glad to see someone's awake!" Off he went until the sounds of "Sold!" and another loud bang marked the end of the sale.

As the hours went by, our hunger and thirst became greater. No one checked on us, and we could only stand helplessly in the pen.

At about mid-day, the auctioneer made an announcement.

"Okay, we're starting the loose horses, now. This is a mare. She has a brand that looks like a bar S. Who'll give me five?" And off he went until we heard, "Sold! Two hundred!"

"Meat price. Bouvrey, probably. Poor girl. She looked like a nice little mare." A woman's voice sounded sad, but resigned.

One after the other, the horses in the pens near us were released and driven down the aisle to a corridor that led to the auction pit. No longer did we hear the excited sounds of many voices and many bidders. Now, the bidding had slowed, and buyers were fewer. They sounded almost nonchalant, the auctioneer's efforts perfunctory. The hum of the crowd was lower, as the morning buyers had begun to leave. The meat buyers remained, waiting to pick up bargains.

Suddenly, I heard a metallic creak as the gate to our pen swung open. I froze. But they had not come for me. Instead, they smacked Buster in the rump to drive him out, and I could hear him anxiously trotting down the aisle.

In the distance, I heard the auctioneer.

"...Sorrel gelding...Who'll give me five?" The auctioneer's voice rolled on, but bidding was slow and unenthusiastic.

"Sold! One hundred fifty."

Almost immediately, the gate swung open again, and I could feel the men around me. I was ushered out and given a smack to get moving.

I could not see where I was going, but I could feel and sense the sides of the aisle, so I knew in which direction to walk. As I walked, the voices became louder until I was almost upon them. I knew instinctively that I was nearly surrounded by a large group of people, and I could tell that the lights were very bright. I hesitated, afraid to move.

Suddenly, I felt a painful blow to my rump, and I reflexively bolted forward to escape. Almost immediately, I had the wind knocked out of me—I had run full speed into a wall not twenty feet away. I grunted in pain but, still panicked, turned and ran forward only to crash again, head first, into another wall. I staggered a few steps, disoriented and in pain.

"Folks this pony appears to be blind. Who'll give me a hundred?" The auctioneer's voice rolled on. "Fifty, who'll give fifty…ten…five dollars…three dollars…just one dollar, folks. One dollar. No one? Okay, take him out of here."

I was led out and down through the aisle, back to my pen. Now, I was alone. My head throbbed, and my throat was parched. It had been a whole day without water or food.

As the afternoon wore on, the last horses were sold. I could hear them being loaded into the large trailers amid shouting and blows. As the trucks pulled away and people began to leave, silence fell on the auction house and back lot. In distant pens, I heard the few remaining horses moving around quietly. As darkness fell, I stood alone in my pen. For the first time, I thought I might die.

The next morning arrived, even more cheerless and cold than the one before it. Throughout the morning, I heard voices of men casually finishing up details of the previous day's business. I could no longer feel the hours passing. I simply stood with my head down, weak and resigned to whatever might happen.

Chapter 11

The Miracle

"The owner never picked him up."

I heard the faint sound of men's voices. They grew louder as the men came closer, and I could hear their footsteps approaching on the concrete.

"I'll take him, but if you don't mind giving me the owner's phone number, I'd like to give him a call to find out a little more about him. Poor old guy. Nothing but ribs underneath that coat," he lamented. For the first time in a long time, I felt a tiny spark of hope.

The gate creaked as it swung open. The men approached, and one of them gently slid a halter over my head. As I waited for him to tell me what to do, he gave my neck a scratch and then snapped a lead onto the halter. Feeling the pressure of the lead, I walked out beside the men, and we set off down the aisle.

Outside, a trailer was waiting for us. I left the auction house not knowing where I was going but relieved to be going away from that horrible place.

Mr. Bowersox abandoned at the auction

As the trailer pulled to a stop, I could smell other horses. We walked into the paddock, where I joyfully discovered that the ground was covered with grass. And to my great relief, I was given a bucket of water to drink. I drank until I could drink no more, and I began to feel better, though I was still weak.

The paddock was enclosed by wire fence. There were no other

horses within it, but I quickly discovered friendly equine neighbors on the other side. So I was not lonely. Debbie, the woman who owned the farm, was kind and gentle. She gave me soft grain and fresh water and talked to me reassuringly.

"You need a name. What do you look like? Let's see. How about Sprinkles? That doesn't seem quite right."

Debbie deliberated this important question, but she left without a final decision. Over the next several days, I heard other names being considered. None of them seemed to resonate with Debbie. Indeed, none of them resonated with me, either. But so many names had come and gone, and I had more important things to think about. I had nearly starved and needed to eat. The sum of my attention was focused on food, and it was too delicious for words.

Then one day, she said it. .

"Good Morning, Mr. Bowersox!"

I tilted my head to listen. Mr. Bowersox. Yes, that was exactly right. My caretaker scratched my neck.

"You'll be the next big thing on American Idol in the rescued pony category," she laughed.

But I knew that name was right. I was Mr. Bowersox, and I was beginning to remember that I was a good boy, and I was also brave. Yes, that was right.

Shortly after his rescue in Montana, Mr. Bowersox's caretaker, Virginia, grooms him and examines him for injuries or signs of illness. She placed a mask on his face to protect his eyes from sun, wind, and dust, all of which can cause irritation.

As the days turned into weeks, I continued to improve. At one point, a veterinarian visited to discuss my condition with Debbie.

"He has Cushing's disease and will need to have daily medication."

In the days after the visit, my appetite mysteriously disappeared.

I had been an enthusiastic eater after my bout of starvation, but now I picked at my feed without much interest. Debbie tried her best to encourage me, but I simply was not hungry. I was becoming thinner again.

My stay with Debbie would not be long. A few weeks after my arrival, I was again loaded into the trailer. I had hardly gotten to know my caretaker or my neighbors, but I was grateful to this woman for her kindness. She told me to be good and promised that I would be okay. For some reason, I believed her.

We did not travel far. When the trailer came to a stop, I recognized a kind and familiar voice. It was Jeff, the man who rescued me from the auction. I also heard a second voice, the voice of a woman I would come to know as Virginia.

"Well, hello, Mr. Bowersox!" I introduced myself. Yes, I am Mr. Bowersox. I am strong and brave and very clever. I was greeted warmly and had my back and neck rubbed. I found myself the subject of Jeff and Virginia's concerned attention. The pair examined me carefully; they worried about my weight.

"Let's take him off the medication to see if that improves his appetite."

Within a day or two, my old appetite was back, and I ate with gusto. I began to feel better again. Jeff and Virginia brushed me and rubbed my neck and face. They fed me soft grain and provided fresh water and lots of company. They became my best friends, coming out every day to take care of me. They didn't even mind much when I ate their rose bush, which smelled intoxicating and tasted delicious.

But I knew I could not stay. Jeff and Virginia had saved my life, but they were not able to keep me. I could hear them talking as they gave me fresh feed and water.

"I've sent emails to a dozen different rescues, but we don't seem to be getting much of a response."

"Even the blind horse sanctuary doesn't seem to have any interest in taking him."

The two talked as I ate, and Virginia softly scratched my back and withers.

I continued to gain weight. My coat began to lose the long, matted clumps, which were replaced by softer, healthier hair. I had more energy now, too, and I started to feel like my old self.

"It looks like White Bird Appaloosa Horse Rescue will take him, but they need to free up some space. And they are a long way off, in Virginia. We would need to get him there." I was sad to hear this news, as I had become very fond of Jeff and Virginia. But there was a hopeful tone in their voices, and I had no choice but to trust them.

A large trailer rolled onto the property. Jeff and Virginia helped load items into the back.

"This is a really nice rig. He is going to travel in style."

"All of his care items are in this box. Don't forget to give them to the rescue. We've also brought you some extra hay."

I walked up to the trailer as Jeff and Virginia said their goodbyes. I would miss these two. They were the first people in a very long time who were sad to see me go.

"You be a good boy."

Chapter 12

On The Road

I was led into a large stall in the center of the trailer. I had been in many trailers over the years, but this was the first time I had been in such an enclosure. It was roomy and bright. There was water and fresh hay, and I could tell immediately that I had neighbors. One of these was a very anxious young mare who paced back and forth but seemed to calm down when I stood near her. She became my traveling companion over the next several days.

As the trailer pulled away, I noticed how smooth and comfortable it was. Rather than the usual creaky, bumpy trailer, this one seemed to glide across the ground. I settled down to eat my hay, occasionally feeling my nervous neighbor start at some unexpected sound. I tried to comfort her. The trailer rocked gently as we traveled.

We drove south and east, across long, rolling highways. We would drive for hours, and then the drivers would stop and let us rest, giving us fresh water, feed, and hay. Sometimes we stopped in locations with abundant activity. We could hear the sound of music and smell food in the air. Vehicles came and went amid the smells of diesel fumes and gasoline; voices laughed and joked. People walked past the trailer, sometimes trying to peek in and see who was inside. We smelled cigarettes and coffee and sometimes alcohol, mixed with the warm smell of tarmac in the sun.

At other times, we pulled into quiet lots with little activity. At night, we heard large semis roll in and park, their tired occupants taking a break, as we were. After a few hours, they pulled away again, leaving little sign that they had ever been there. We would be off again, too, in the still hours of early morning.

The journey alternated between bustling towns and cities, dense with the sounds of heavy traffic and the smells of industries and restaurants, and open farmland, with its moist smells of fields and animals. The air became hotter and drier, then more humid. We crossed mountains, valleys, and plains.

The trailer gently swayed while we ate our hay and took in the sounds and smells. I periodically put my nose over the partition to check on my nervous traveling companion, who stayed close to me. The miles became hundreds and then hundreds became thousands. I had never traveled so far in my life.

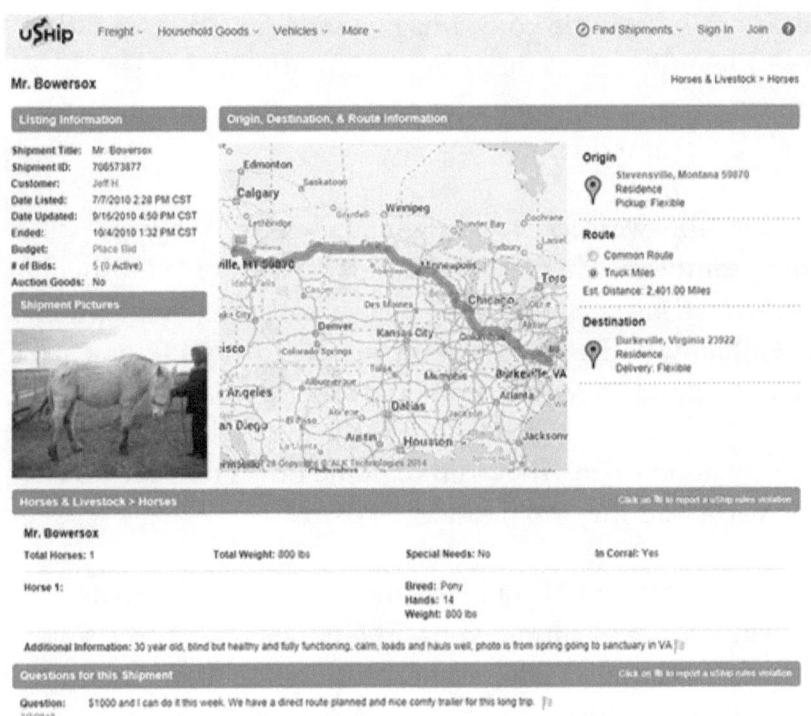

Mr. Bowersox's Journey began in western Montana. He travelled more than 2,400 miles in the course of three days to reach the White Bird Appaloosa Horse Rescue in central Virginia. His trip took him across most of the United States, and he travelled through Montana, North Dakota, Minnesota, Wisconsin, Indiana, Illinois, Ohio, West Virginia, and Virginia

"Okay, I've given them an ETA. They'll be waiting for us."

The drivers were taking a morning break to give us water and hay and let us rest. They stood leaning against the side of the trailer, drinking cups of coffee.

"This is one lucky little pony. Imagine sending him over 2,000 miles. They must think he is pretty important." I listened to the men talk and wondered if, indeed, there was someone who thought I was important.

That day, the weather was bright and clear. We were still heading southeast. We crossed mountains, then rolled through foothills and lower, softer hills, then across long stretches of straight highway. Large trucks continued to rumble past us. My companion had settled down and seemed far more relaxed.

"They are good to go. They said to come down past the house to the barns and they would meet us there."

The trailer slowed, and I could feel that we had left the highway. I smelled farms and spring crops. The trailer slowed to a stop, then turned sharply. I felt and heard the gravel drive beneath us as it dipped, climbed uphill, then started back down. As we approached the hill, I heard the sound of hoof beats racing toward us, and I recognized the sounds of horses greeting a trailer. I was being welcomed with enthusiasm, and I could smell horses all around me.

Chapter 13

Starting Over

We finally came to a stop. Nearby, I could hear curious horses jostling to see who had arrived. The driver hopped out of the truck, and I heard voices. I could only wait. I wondered if there would be someone to take care of me. I wondered if they would have food.

"Can I turn around in here?"

"Sure, just back up a little past the L-barn and you've got tons of room." The voices circled the trailer.

"He's been my best passenger. That little mare in there was throwing a fit. He was a real help in keeping her settled down. Cool as a cucumber, that one."

"Let's get his things out, first. There's a box here with his name on it and some hay, I think."

Doors opened, and I could hear the sounds of items being

unloaded.

"Look! It says 'Mr. Bowersox, from Montana to Virginia!'" a woman chuckled. "Aww!"

The side door opened, and all of a sudden the stall was filled with light. I blinked and tried to focus. I could see almost nothing, only green expanse and some type of building.

"Well, hello, Mr. Bowersox!"

My heart leapt. They knew! They knew who I was! I had been Chief, Jack, Sam, Chico, and Lightening. I had been a nameless, blind pony in an auction pen. But from over 2,000 miles away, they knew.

The voices were soft and low. I felt a hand on my halter, and I was led slowly out of the trailer. I stepped down the ramp carefully to a level grassy area. Several people stood around me. I looked around and tried to see as best I could, stood up straight, and introduced myself:

I AM Mr. Bowersox, and I am pleased to meet you. I am strong and brave and very clever. I am kind to children, and I am a good boy.

A hand gently scratched my neck. "You've had a long trip, old man."

I began to walk with the small group of people to the end of a long building, around the corner, and then into an aisle way.

I could hear and smell horses everywhere. I was led into a stall and could see only darkness because of my vision. But I could smell shavings and hay and fresh water. I could also smell a mare nearby.

Hushed voices came from the direction of the stall door. "I hope he likes his new neighbor."

"More to the point, I hope she likes him. She hasn't liked anyone at all so far—human or equine."

"Yeah, but she might at least tolerate another blind pony. Worth a try."

I circled around to get my bearings. The stall was big, and I had plenty of room. As I felt my way around it, I realized that one wall had been lowered so that it was close to the height of a paddock fence, and I could lean my head over the side. As I did, I heard a most amazing sound: a small, throaty chuckle from the other side of the low wall.

"Hmm'mm'mm'mm!"

I picked up my ears to hear better. Could this be possible? Could I be mistaken? Within seconds, a tiny muzzle was breathing into mine in absolute delight.

"I just don't believe that."

"Will you look at that?"

"No way! She hates everybody!"

But the joy in her voice was unmistakable. I returned her affection with a low nicker of my own. She wasn't Maggie, but she was lovely and sweet and beautiful. And she was thrilled to see me.

Her name was Allison. She was my age, nearly forty years old—a tiny Shetland pony mix with markings just like mine. She was found wandering aimlessly in a field, starved and very sick. Strangers had abandoned the pony on the property, and the property owners were horrified when they discovered the neglected animal.

When they found her, Allison was emaciated and loaded with parasites. Her few remaining teeth were infected and painful, and her nose ran constantly from a sinus infection. Though she was already blind, one eye was so severely damaged that it required removal.

The property owners wanted to put her down. She was clearly suffering from the extensive neglect that she had endured. But the veterinarian called to perform the euthanasia saw spirit and a spark of defiance in her. The vet asked if Allison could be rehomed, instead, if she provided veterinary care for free.

So, Allison had come to live at White Bird the year before. Under the rescue's care, she regained her physical condition. But despite the kind treatment by staff and volunteers, Allison had no confidence in horses or people.

I learned about her by listening to the casual conversations of volunteers around the barn. They could tell that she had been trained at some time in her life. But she was grumpy and sour and would kick out like lightening when her hooves were being trimmed. She disliked being handled, and her tiny body cringed when she was groomed. Some event in her life, one that we would never know, had destroyed her trust in anyone and everyone. Except me.

Only she knew what she recognized in me. She was loving and affectionate, as if welcoming a dear, long-lost friend. I had the best companion I could possibly have wished for. Wherever I went, she was there with me. Wherever she went, I followed. We groomed each other and ate together on opposite sides of the low partition. At night, I slept with my head bent over the partition so that I could be close to her. When we grazed, we stood as close together as two ponies could stand. Whenever we were separated, we called out to locate each other. She was my girl, and I simply adored her.

Mr. Bowersox and Allison in adjacent stalls

The rescue staff and volunteers were very kind to me. They brought me soft pelleted food that had been soaked to make it easier to eat. I was also given "chopped forage," which I love. I am a slow eater because of my teeth, but I had company. As I slowly ate my food, Allison slowly ate hers beside me. Her teeth were bad, too.

Allison and I had our own special paddock. We were seniors and blind and couldn't compete with the stronger, sighted horses. And we were small in comparison to the big guys in the field. We were close to many other horses, but we spent our days in the safety of our paddock and its green shelter. When it rained, we stood inside together and chewed hay, looking out from under the overhang.

Mr. Bowersox and the love of his life

I had a special job at the rescue, and it was an important one. When visitors came out, I was the best pony for teaching them about horses. This is because I am gentle and friendly, and I always stood politely while small children and timid adults learned all about us. They brushed my coat until it was soft and clean, and I nuzzled them, looking for treats. Sometimes, I heard "Hey, Mr. B.!" or just "Howdy, B.!" and I knew they were talking to me. I would come up to the stall and put my nose out for a pat or rub.

The rescue's veterinarian provided medical treatment for

us. One day, he was called to examine me, and I could hear concern in his voice.

"It is cancer. It looks like squamous cell. See here?" Everyone seemed to be inspecting my belly.

"We can try to remove it and hope it doesn't return."

Standing in the afternoon sun, I felt the sting of a bee and then drifted off. I awoke feeling stiff and sore. The rescue staff kept a close eye on me for a while and kept me very clean. When the stitches were removed, the veterinarian's voice was hopeful. It looked good, he said. And so it was.

About a year after I arrived, I sensed that something unusual was about to happen. The rescue staff had tidied up the tack room and brushed my coat until it was shiny. It seemed that we were about to have visitors. The voices began at the top of the driveway, as they generally did when people approached. As they got louder, I began to recognize them, and my heart leapt.

"Well, hello, Mr. Bowersox!" It was Jeff and Virginia! All the way from Montana! They threw their arms around me, and I leaned into them. They scratched me and talked to me, and I was so happy to see them. My old friends had not forgotten me, and I have never forgotten them, either.

A visit from Jeff and Virginia

As the seasons changed and years passed, our lives were peaceful. Allison and I were happy. People were kind to us, and we had plenty of good food and fresh water. But the world is an uncertain place, and this too, would not last forever.

I had noticed for months that Allison was sometimes unsteady on her feet. It began with a slight problem with her balance. This was not unexpected in ponies as old as we were. We were far older than most horses ever live to be, or even most ponies. At our ages, some things are just to be expected. But Allison's problem became worse.

I tried not to notice. I told myself it wasn't too serious and thought she probably was just a little stiff. We both had some arthritis. I tried to convince myself that this was no big deal.

As Allison's condition worsened, I simply slowed down so that she could keep up, and I waited while she steadied herself. But I knew she wasn't feeling well. She was not always hungry and was quieter than she had been. The staff and volunteers at the rescue also knew that something was wrong. They watched her carefully, too.

One day, it became clear that she was in great pain. She could hardly keep her balance, and she shivered and sweated. She would not eat. The veterinarian was called.

I waited on my side of the partition, listening intently as he completed his exam. He addressed the rescue staff in a voice of sad resignation.

"I wish I had a better answer, but there is nothing more we can do for her."

"I'm sorry, old girl," said her caretaker, his voice strained and sad.

I knew the second Allison left us. One moment she was there. In the next, all that she was—her memories, her pain, her love and her defiance—was gone, leaving only emptiness in the place where her spirit had been.

The loss of my beloved Allison was devastating. The pain was deep and visceral, and every moment, I still hoped for her return. But I never called out for her again. She was gone.

It took time, but eventually I stopped listening for her tiny whinny whenever I was out of sight. I ate my meals in silence, knowing that there was no one to share them with on the other side of our partition. On sunny days, I dozed alone in the paddock, knowing there was no one beside me, listening to me breathe. I learned to live without her. I never learned not to miss her.

Chapter 14

My Life, These Days

The crisp air is now filled with the sounds of volunteers, wheelbarrows, and feed tubs. Around me are the thumps and whooshes of afternoon chores. I can hear the unmistakable sound of grain pouring into buckets in the tack room, as dinner is being prepared. I love that sound. The soft clip-clop of hooves in the aisle way tells me that horses are being brought in for their evening meal, as others are led out to their pastures. Farther down the aisle, a voice speaks softly to sweet Pebbles, the big blind mare, because she is anxious about her companion, a miniature horse named Belle, who has been taken out ahead of her. Pebbles circles in her stall, then pauses and listens intently. She knows she should go next.

"Hi, pretty girl! Ready to go out?"

On the other side of the barn, the little Welsh pony, Oreo, whinnies to get someone's attention. Oreo is as old as I am and is the smartest pony I have ever met. He has almost no teeth and must eat pellets soaked into mush. But he has made many friends. Sometimes, he just calls out for people to come over and pet him. He had his own people once, but somehow he lost them.

Today, I have a home and an important job and people who love me. I have a lot of company and a best friend named Mona, who is also blind. I have good food and a warm stall and friends to scratch my withers. But I still miss my Allison, and I move slowly these days, for I am very old.

Mr. B Christmas 2012

The sound of footsteps tells me that someone familiar is approaching.

"Hello, Mr. B." A hand rubs my brow and scratches my neck. I check to see if my friend Tom has brought a treat. But he proceeds down the aisle, and I know my food will soon arrive. I put my nose out to see if I can smell it. Then, I wait.

The years have flown by, leaving me with few dreams and many memories. I have known many people and animals, losing ones I cared about and ones I was glad to escape. Sometimes, they reappear without warning, in a smell or a sound, or the gentle nuzzle of a friend, only to disappear again, vanishing like spirits. I have known hunger and its dark companion, fear, and I have grieved the loss of my loved ones. Those memories, too, suddenly arise unwelcome but are quickly chased away by the sound of my feed bucket being filled, or the caress of a small hand on my cheek.

I have learned many things. I have seen kindness and cruelty, often from the same person. The people I loved most were the most painful to lose, and some of them sent me off without a second thought. Those who loved me allowed me to slip away, unable or unwilling to come back for me. A man who meant me no harm caused me great suffering, unaware that he was doing so. The man I feared most left me to die, frightened and alone. I never understood what I had done to make him so angry. Strangers reached out to save my life, even though we had never met, and they had no reason to help me.

I have learned that cows are loving, goats are smart, and children can be as cruel or kind as they wish. But there is much about the world that I will never understand.

These days, I just doze in the sun, thinking about long-ago places and things. I wonder where Catherine is, and whether she ever thinks of me. I loved her very much. As I drift off to sleep, sometimes I am back in my mountains, racing down the valley with my friend, feeling the wind in my face. I am strong and brave and clever. I am Mr. Bowersox.

Chapter 15

Two Thousand Miles Away

The sound of heels on the vinyl floor echoed as she walked down the hall. She turned the key in the lock and then switched on the lights, which hummed with a blue, florescent glow. She hung her coat over the hook and set her purse under the desk. Reaching up, she switched on the lights above her cubicle. Through the window, the sky had a pale cast to it, almost white. She turned on the small radio sitting on the bookshelf above her.

"…Mountain Music 107 FM, all your favorites…"

It was early. She had work to do, and there was nothing worth staying home for. Molly the cat would still be sleeping on the end of her bed. There were accounts to catch up on and emails to answer. She began to organize the papers on the desk. The radio in the background droned away.

"…From the National Weather Service…" The man's voice caught her ear. "This is going to be a heavy early-season snowfall, so don't let it catch you off guard. It's going to be a mess out there, so give yourself plenty of time and be prepared for possible accidents and delays."

She sighed. She would have to leave early to beat rush hour. She might pick up a salad on the way home. As she looked up at the window, a few fat snowflakes drifted lazily by.

She used to love the snow. Her mother would bundle them up like short, fat ticks in snow suits and rubber boots, then help them roll the snow into large balls to make equally fat snowmen. They had giggled and whooped as they made silly faces out of carrots and stones. They played until their hands were frozen and they were too exhausted to take another step in the deep snow. She smiled faintly.

But things changed after the accident, and winter had never been the same. Pa was too serious and too busy to make snowmen. And then there was that one time. Her mind went back over thirty years. She had been out riding her pony, and they had gotten lost in the snow. He had brought her home safely during one of the area's worst blizzards. It was so cold. What ever happened to the little guy? Probably died years ago. What was his name? She snapped back to the present and finished straightening the papers. She repositioned the sign on her desk:

"Catherine Hamby, Accounts Receivable."

The steady clack of the keyboard was the only sound for a long time.

About The Author

Jorg Huckabee-Mayfield has a BA in environmental science, an MSCE in civil engineering from the University of Virginia, and an MPA from George Mason University. She is the co-founder and current President of the White Bird Appaloosa Horse Rescue. Since 2003, White Bird has rescued Appaloosas and other horses in urgent need, also providing for the care and treatment of blind horses. In 2014, White Bird was awarded the Carole Noon Award for Sanctuary Excellence from the Global Federation of Animal Sanctuaries. Jorg lives with her family on the rescue farm in Burkeville, VA.

Jorg Huckabee-Mayfield and her friend Folly

www.ingramcontent.com/pod-product-compliance
Lightning Source LLC
Chambersburg PA
CBHW030344030726
47499CB00003B/890